Mausoleum

WILLIAM PHILLIPS

Second Edition August 2016

ISBN: 978-0692765913

Printed in the United States of America

Acknowledgements

I'd like to thank all of my family and friends for your support over the years. If it wasn't for each and every one of you I wouldn't be the person I am today.

All proceeds from this book will be donated to the *Addison-Needs-To-Go-To-College Fund.*

To Trooper Bill
You taught me the value of reading at a young age. You don't get enough credit for all of the things you've done for us. This one is for you!

Mausoleum

1

The frost formed an icy barrier around the cheap aluminum window frame. Cold seeped in around the edges and seemingly through the flimsy glass. Ice formed tiny droplets at the bottom of the pane, giving the entire room a cave-like feeling.

The cold didn't stop there. The entire room seemed to have a blue tint and the slightest hint of human breath would create a dense fog. Adding to the cold feeling, the room was nearly devoid of furniture. There was a single desk on the far side of the room, strategically placed as far away from the frosty window as possible.

A slight oak scent permeated throughout the room from the decades-old desk. There were chips and nicks all over its legs. Splinters jutted from the frayed corners attempting to mirror the spiked icicles below the window. In contrast to the ragged legs, the top appeared smooth. It had been recently sanded down and a calendar framed the corners. The calendar was nearly empty except for a few scratch marks near the bottom.

The inhabitant behind the desk was talking the phone. As she spoke, she twirled the curled cord around her finger. Her voice was soft, but assertive.

There was a small filing cabinet and a few stacks of papers lying on the floor around the room. Directly across from the desk, there was a thin door that led to another small room. A lone voice was coming from behind the door. It didn't seem to bother the inhabitant at the desk. She spoke a little louder so the caller on the phone could her hear.

"Yes," she said. "I will have someone there."

She squinted her eyes while trying to hear the voice on the other end. The voice behind the door was getting louder and louder.

"How many days are we budgeted for?"

The voice behind the door was getting

louder. She couldn't make out what it was saying, but it was obvious the voice was on the phone as well.

"How many?" She repeated.

She couldn't hear a thing now. The voice was overpowering her soft tone.

"Hold on," she said with her pleasant tone she had worked so hard to perfect over the years.

She pushed the mute button on the primitive phone, and out of habit still put her hand over the lower end of the receiver.

"Jeff," she yelled in the direction of the door. "I'm trying to book a job here."

Suddenly the door flew open and Jeff stuck his head out of the crack.

"I'm sorry Sandy," he whispered, pulling his cell phone away from his ear.

This was the first time that Jeff had actually looked at Sandy this morning. Her short brown curls were beginning to fall into her eyes. That usually didn't happen until much later in the day, but the last few months had been rough on everyone.

The construction business had fallen in recent years. Several new competitors had moved into the area and began giving lower bids on almost every project. Jeff struggled to stay afloat. He was forced to lay off nearly his entire crew. He promised them all he would call them back someday, but he knew deep down that day might never come.

Many of his old crew had gone to work for the competition. Jeff didn't mind. He didn't see this as a betrayal. He knew these men. These were good men. They had to do what they had to do to feed their families. It hurt Jeff more to know that he couldn't keep paying them than it did to know they were working for the very companies that put him in this position.

Sandy was still staring him down. He knew his voice was loud and carried through the entire construction trailer, driving Sandy a little crazy. Sandy threw her weight from one side of the chair to the other as she reached back for the phone. Jeff watched and couldn't help but notice how much she had changed throughout the years.

She was once a young and beautiful woman. Jeff had once thought about asking her out in college, but she soon began dating his best friend, Alex. The three of them quickly became inseparable and Sandy became like a sister to him. Now, Sandy sat, hunched in the chair like she was carrying the weight of the entire company on her shoulders. She was 5'7" but looked much smaller in the oversized chair.

Jeff watched her once-soft hand, which had become hardened and calloused over the years, press the mute button and continue talking into the phone.

He ducked back into his office and

quickly ended his phone call. By the time he emerged again into the cold main office of the construction trailer, Sandy had finished her phone call and was jotting notes onto the calendar on the desk. Jeff approached the desk but Sandy did not look up until she finished writing.

"I booked a job," Sandy said without meeting Jeff's eyes.

Jeff looked directly at Sandy but was unable to meet her gaze.

"Great. Is it the new sports center they are building in Youngstown? My bid was rock bottom. There's no way Davis could have beat us on that one." Jeff was excited.

"No," Sandy said briefly, dashing his hopes. "It's the clean up job."

Jeff looked confused. Sandy looked up at his face, but still avoided eye contact.

"Don't you remember?" She asked. "I told you about this one last week. The owner contacted me directly."

Jeff was still puzzled. It wasn't like him to forget a job, especially now, when they were so few and far between.

Sandy looked into Jeff's eyes for the first time. "Do you want the job or not?" She used the same soft but firm tone that she had used on the phone.

"Yes, of course we do." Jeff blushed. Sandy knew he wasn't in any position to turn down a job, even if he hadn't remembered bidding on it in the first place.

"Okay. Give me a few hours and I will line up the crew."

Jeff protested, "Sandy, you don't need to do that. I can take care of--"

She cut him off. "Don't be silly, I still work here. I will take care of everything."

***

Sandy gave in to the cold shortly after lunch. She couldn't take it any more and switched on the small space heater and placed it carefully under the wooden desk. She sat as close to it as she could to try to gather what little heat it was throwing off.

She spent the rest of the day making phone calls. She knew Jeff's staff like she knew her family. No. They were her family. She had been working at Crane Construction for nearly 20 years. It was her first job out of college and had become a second home to her over the years. It killed her more than it hurt Jeff when he began to let them go. They were like her children. She had watched them grow up over the years. Some matured into supervisors and project managers. Some moved on to bigger and better things after their construction days were over. Some stayed just as immature as they day she met them. They were the children that Sandy never had.

It was hard for her to see them go, and now there were only 10 left on the payroll. Jeff had made a few wrong decisions about who to let go, but Sandy never felt it was her place to butt in.

She took great pride in being able to make the calls today. She always felt a sense of accomplishment when she was able to call and offer someone work, even if it was a pretty crappy job this time. Only a few days work. But still, it was the dead of winter, and few other jobs were on the horizon until spring.

After hanging up the phone with her first employee, Sandy began to smirk. She was very pleased with herself. By the time she had finished her fourth phone call, she was nearly giddy.

Everyone Sandy called greeted her warmly, and thanked her for the opportunity. There were a few that she hadn't spoken to in months. As she sat at her desk smiling, Jeff came barreling out of his small office and invaded her space.

He didn't say a word as his tall, lanky frame cleared a pile of papers from a lone chair and dragged it opposite Sandy's desk. His hair was closely shaved to his head to hide that it was starting to thin. It was speckled with white and beginning to lose some of its shine. Sandy could see the outline of a tank top underneath his t-shirt. Layered over his t-shirt was a flannel shirt that looked fresh out of the package, still showing the creases from where it was folded.

Jeff looked at the ground briefly and then glanced up at Sandy. She was not avoiding his gaze this time. She was looking directly at him. Something about her attitude had changed. She had started to once again show a spark of life. It was a sharp contrast to the hollow shell of a woman he had seen earlier.

They looked at each other for what felt like hours, but was in reality only a few moments. Jeff spoke first.

"Sandy, is there anything I can do?"

"No," she said softly. "I understand."

Both parties knew exactly what they other was talking about. Sandy noticed the clock on the wall for the first time today. It was nearly 5 o'clock.

"If there was any other way, I would choose it in a heartbeat." Jeff said, trying to keep any emotion hidden beneath his flannel.

"Don't worry about me. You've known me for what? 25 years? I always find a way to pull through."

"You do," Jeff said, knowing she was tougher than him. "Even last year when…"

Jeff trailed off. He couldn't think of any words to say. He met Sandy's eyes again and it was obvious that he didn't have to finish what he was saying. She knew exactly what he meant.

She looked down for a second, took a deep breath, and met his eyes again.

"I have you all set for Monday's job." She wanted to change the subject.

Even though Jeff wasn't great at picking up social clues, this one jumped out at him like a jackrabbit.

"Great. What time? How many?" he asked.

"You need to be there at 7 AM. All of the crew have been notified. There are five of you."

"Thanks Sandy. I really appreciate it."

"Don't be silly." Sandy said. She noticed the clock again as it struck 5 o'clock.

She, too, had been a victim of the lay offs at Crane Construction. She was now officially off the clock. "Just think of it as my final act!"

2

Amanda sat in the car. The warm, dry wind blowing from the vents in front of her did nothing to cure the chill. The thermometer on her beat up old Chevy Cavalier said it was 23 degrees outside. It was 6:45AM and she was early. She pulled her hand out of a thin, worn-leather glove and began to flip through the radio stations. She paused at one announcing the weather.

"High today is a chilly 29 degrees. Don't

forget, all local schools are running on a two hour delay because of those wind chills that are currently below zero," the announcer said, surely to the delight of all the children in the state. Amanda shivered as she quickly pulled the leather glove back on to her freezing hand.

She glanced up at the rear view mirror and caught a glimpse of her face. Her cheeks were puffy with dark circles framing her piercing blue eyes. Her hair was dirty blonde and pulled back in a pony tail. There were a few highlights that remained from a months old dye job.

Amanda was beautiful, but looked like no one had bothered to tell her. Other than the highlights she had never really given much though to her appearance. She could never understand how other women could take hours primping each morning. Amanda had the 10 minute morning routine down pat. She would hit the alarm clock, hop up directly into the steaming hot shower. This morning had taken a few extra moments since it was so bone chillingly cold outside.

After the shower, her hair would be immediately pulled back into a pony tail to air dry. If she was feeling particularly ambitious, she would put on some lip gloss. Most days she left the house with no makeup at all.

Today was one of those days. Amanda always had to be early for work. Her alarm went off at 6:15AM this morning. She rolled out of bed, perfectly executed the 10-minute morning routine, fed her dog, and was out of the house by 6:35.

She was lucky. The site where they were called out to today was only 10 minutes from her house, putting her a good 15 minutes early. In fact, the car hadn't even warmed up properly on the drive over, which led to her still trying to find some warmth while she waited for the others.

She glanced away from her own reflection in the mirror and focused on the building she was parked in front of. It towered to nearly three stories and was the width of two football fields. From where Amanda was sitting, it was nearly impossible to tell how far back the building went, but she guessed it was at least as long as it was wide.

The roof came to a slight peak in the middle and two perfect white columns framed the only door. There was not a single window on the building and that gave Amanda another chill, which felt entire different from the cold.

The entire façade of the building was white marble. Amanda couldn't tell if that was merely a thin outside coating, or if the building itself was solid marble.

Amanda wasn't sure if it was the creepy building or the bone chilling cold, but a wave of panic slowly crept over her. She looked around the parking lot for another sign of life. The sun was just beginning to rise and shadows lined the parking lot.

The trees that lined the lot swayed slowly in the cold winter breeze. Even though they held no leaves, the trees still managed to form a solid barrier down the side of the parking lot, parallel to the sterile building, and dancing around the rear far from Amanda's eye sight.

As she began to look around, she noticed for the first time that the trees formed a perfectly square box around the parking lot and the building. The only break was for the small entrance Amanda pulled into only a few minutes ago.

Sunlight broke through the tops of the trees behind the building, nearly blinding Amanda if she tried to look forward. It created a halo around the cold white building and Amanda had to place her hand in front of her face to protect her eyes from the glare.

She squinted to try to get a better look at the building. Darting quickly from left to right in front of her car, something moved and shook Amanda to her core. She wasn't the nervous type. There was something about this building that made her feel uneasy.

Amanda squinted harder and quickly darting her eyes left to right and then back again trying to catch a glimpse of the figure moving outside. Was it a deer? It wasn't uncommon this time of year for a deer to be out in the woods wondering around, looking for food.

She couldn't see anything. The chill she was experiencing from the cold just moments before was nothing compared to the unease of being alone and helpless with someone just outside the car.

But, Amanda wasn't helpless. She was strong willed and rational and something like this, an unconfirmed fear, was not usually enough to rattle her. She took a deep breath and opened her eyes wide. The sun was not going to stop her from getting a good look around.

The sun was nearly blinding but Amanda finally got a good look at the parking lot. Nothing but trees to her left. Nothing but trees to her right. The lot was empty. She was sure of it. She turned around to check behind her. There was nothing. Out of habit she even checked the backseat. Surely she would have known if someone had opened the door, allowing a wave of frosty air in. But, it made her feel better to know she was indeed alone.

She relaxed a little in the seat. She realized she hadn't been breathing. How long had that been going on? She let out a deep breath and drew another in. Her rational side reminded her that the doors were still unlocked.

Amanda focused her attention on the lock button and slowly reached a gloved hand towards it. She was merely an inch away when the passenger door of the car flew open. She immediately tensed and sat straight up in her seat. She wanted to scream but her vocal cords would not cooperate. A small grunt escaped her throat as she willed herself to pierce the cold with a scream.

She jerked her head to the right to see what was tumbling through her door. The sun had reached the top of the trees to her right also which made everything in front of her seem like a hazy bad dream. She couldn't focus her eyes, but she could distinctly see the shadow of a human being lunging towards her. She lifted her hands to defend herself when her eyes caught the first glimpse of the human's face. It was a man. It was a face she recognized. It was Andrew.

"Hey," Andrew said, jumping into the passenger's seat and closing the door behind him.

She willed her body to relax when she saw the sight of her co-worker, but it would not listen. Andrew noticed he had startled her.

"Wow. You're not usually the jumpy type." Andrew said, rubbing his hands in front of the vent to warm them up.

Amanda suddenly felt the tension in her back ease up and she began to relax. Anger filled her face and she reached across the car and gave Andrew a firm slap on the back.

"You scared the hell outta me," she said,

watching him push his long brown hair behind his ear.

Like Amanda, Andrew wasn't exactly you're stereotypical construction worker. Sure, he had what the general public seemed to think of as a "construction attitude." He was laid back, with an *it'll-get-done-when-it-gets-done* way of working. In reality, Amanda never felt the construction business to be like that. She worked her butt off on each and every job and always felt the others around her gave their all as well. Of course, Amanda felt that her all and Andrew's all was completely different. But still, he did try.

Amanda took a long look at Andrew. He had long, wavy brown hair that was the perfect length to tuck behind his ears. Amanda always wondered why he kept it so long when it obviously got in the way so much, especially in a job like this. He looked like he was in his late 20s and had blue eyes that nearly perfect matched her own. He always looked underdressed for every job.

Today he was wearing his usual outfit. A short-sleeved shirt layered on top of a long-sleeved one. It reminded Amanda of childhood television. Today Andrew's shirts are brought to you by the colors green and white. He wore the same pair of dirty jeans most days and complimented it with a black pair of work boots.

Amanda realized that she didn't know

that much about him. He was always very social and charming at work but either guarded (or maybe just uninterested) in talking about his personal life.

"I'm sorry, I--" Amanda cut him off.

"Are you seriously not wearing a jacket? It's the coldest day of the year so far."

"It was only a 10 minute walk," he responded casually.

"You walked here?" Amanda was stunned.

"Sure did. Only live a mile away. This place always gave me the creeps. My friends and I used to sneak down here and party. We broke in a few times and took a look around."

Amanda noticed that the radio in the car was quite loud. She could hear the announcer giving the weather report. "We are expecting quite a bit of snow today. Should start up here in about an hour and we could see as much as 10 to 12 inches before all is said and done."

"Can you believe that?" Andrew asked.

"What?"

"They're always calling for snow. 9 times out of 10 we don't even get anything."

"Not today," Amanda said. "They've been calling for it all week, and it's really coming today."

"If that's the case, I hope we don't get snowed it," Andrew said, with a wink.

This quickly focused Amanda's attention

back to the building in front of her. The sun had disappeared as the building once again appeared dark and menacing. In reality the sun was hiding behind a cloud, but Amanda once again felt a chill running down her spine.

"What is this place?" She asked, not really expecting an answer. Her eyes did not move from the hypnotizing white marble.

"You really don't know what this place is?" Andrew was surprised. Amanda shook her head. "It's a mausoleum."

3

Sandy resisted the urge to pull the covers back over her head and go back to sleep. She awoke at exactly 7 o'clock, which is what her body has been used to for the last 20 years. Her mind, in a cloudy, sleepy haze, willed her to get up, shower, and get ready for work. She had to remind it that she no longer had a job.

The sinking feeling in her stomach was what was telling her to crawl into the warm comfort of her bed. She resisted the urge, threw back the covers, and sat straight up. She was not going to let the lay off affect her any more than it already had. Things had been going tough for Sandy, but she was determined to get out of bed and accomplish everything she wanted to do today.

As her feet hit the cold hardwood floor, she was reminded of the bitter cold that western Pennsylvania had been experiencing over the last few days. The chill of the construction trailer still haunted her and she couldn't seem to get warm enough, now, even days later.

She scurried across the room and entered the adjoining bathroom. She quickly turned on the shower, carefully pushing the faucet to its hottest setting. Steam began to fill the room and Sandy took several deep breaths allowing the warm moist air to fill her lungs and warm her from the inside.

Once the bathroom was an acceptable temperature, Sandy disrobed and jumped in the shower. She stood under the running water and let it wrap her in a cocoon of warmth. Her skin began to turn red from the heat, but Sandy didn't notice. This was the first time in days she felt warm blooded again.

The steam filled the room like a dense fog. It clung to the mirrors, metal shower rod, and anything else it was drawn to. When Sandy finally finished, she threw open the shower curtain and found herself unable to see her towel hanging on the back of the door, only a few feet in front of her.

The towel hung on the back of the door. Through the steam the bathroom's lone light shined above the mirror. The light from the fixture bounced off of the mirror, and under normal circumstances lit up the room nicely. The light struggled through the steam now just as Sandy did.

She blindly reached for it, receiving little help from the light. She felt her hand on the soft plush towel and clutched it as if her life depended on it. She pulled it close and covered her face with it, allowing the lush fabric to embrace her and absorb the excess water that was still dripping from her face.

As she pulled the towel away from her face, she was struck by how dark the room looked. She immediately began to panic as she noticed the light in the bathroom was gone. Did someone switch it off? Did the power go out?

The steam that Sandy felt so comforting only moments again, quickly became menacing. The only light in the entire bathroom was coming from a crack under the door. There were no windows. No night light. Nothing to help her see. The steam only made things worse and Sandy felt as if she was wearing goggles. She wrapped the towel around herself and stepped out of the shower. She made her way through the steam and reached for the doorknob.

She stopped herself inches away from it as her imagination began to run wild. The light switch was just outside the bathroom door on the wall of her bedroom. Was someone out there? Is there something toying with her? Was it just time for the bulb to die? Did the heavy moisture in the air short something out?

This couldn't be happening to her. It must be something completely ordinary. It couldn't be anything sinister.

Sandy took a deep breath. The air was still heavy with moisture and her lungs ached as she tried to breathe in. She thought about how just a few minutes ago the same steam in her bathroom was comforting, warming her skin. Now, she wished it away. She touched the door knob and it perspired. She gripped it firmly to avoid it slipping out of her hand. She readied her other hand.

Her plan was to open the door a crack and flip the light switch back to the on position then slam the door shut again. She slowly turned the door knob. The door creaked in agony as she opened it just enough to slide her hand through the crack. Sandy slowly, carefully reached a hand out and slid it across the door frame onto the smooth paint of the bedroom wall. She slid her hand down the wall but it would not find the light switch.

She took another deep breath to keep from panicking. The cold air that rushed in from the door frame cooled her lungs and allowed her brain a moment of reprieve. She slid her hand again back up looking for the light switch. She half expected a sharp pain to hit her at any moment but nothing came as she made contact with the switch. It was still in the on position.

She quickly calculated in her mind the possible scenarios and settled on one. The power went out. She slid the door open another few inches and pressed her round face in the crack. She looked around the bedroom for any signs to confirm her suspicion. The alarm clock was dim. The table lamp, which she was sure she left on when she fell asleep, was dark.

Sandy pushed open the bathroom door and the steam rushed from behind her disappearing into the cold bedroom air. She walked to her bedside table, pulled out a flashlight, and headed towards the fuse box.

4

Amanda looked down at her watch. It was 7:15. She stood near the door of the mausoleum with her arms crossed trying to stay warm. The entire crew had gathered and they were about to get started, only 15 minutes late. That may be a new record. Amanda looked around at the group.

Directly next to her was Andrew. They continued their conversation in the car until everyone arrived and began gathering in front of the foreboding building. Andrew didn't look cold in the least. Amanda wondered how his thin layered shirts could be warming his body, but he didn't seem to notice. Directly next to Andrew were the twins, Lyle and Kyle.

Amanda never had trouble telling them apart. Kyle wore his naturally brown hair very short and cropped and had a slighter build than his brother. Today, as always, he was wearing his trademark orange hunting jacket. Amanda figured you could probably see it from space it was so bright. Kyle also had a scar on his ear that set him apart from his brother.

Lyle, on the other hand, had bleached his hair so much that it nearly looked white. His tanned skin was a sharp contrast and his arms were nearly as wide as Amanda's neck. He rarely wore anything other than a flannel shirt and carpenter's jeans, and today was no exception. It struck Amanda again. Was she the only one around here who was freezing? Only Kyle came close to being properly dressed for the weather.

Next to the twins was Jeff, Amanda's boss for nearly 10 years. Jeff had given her her first job outside of high school. Amanda hadn't always been the only girl on the crew. There had been others over the years. But she was the only one left on the payroll. Sometimes they came and went as they found other jobs. Sometimes they couldn't take working with the male members of the crew. Amanda had formed bonds with a few of them over the years, but nothing that lasted more than the length of their employment.

Amanda never had a problem with the guys. Some of the women confided in her that they felt the men looked down on them and would even claim they were harassed. If they were, Amanda was oblivious to it. Never once in 10 years had she felt anything but one of the team. She made sure coming in that she would earn their respect, and she did. She worked hard, if not harder than most of them, and Jeff took notice as well. She always called first for nearly every job.

Lyle and Kyle had been around longer than she had. They were all still in the same small town they were born in, and the twins went to high school with Amanda. They were a few years older than her, but the stories that spread about them reached the entire school. They were both womanizers. They were always very charming and Amanda could remember back to when they both still looked identical. It wasn't until after high school that they sought to create their own identities by changing their appearances. Amanda could remember rumors about them swapping places to date each other's girls and the girls being none the wiser.

Andrew, on the other hand, was really the newbie. He'd only been working there a few years and Amanda was as surprised as the rest of the crew. It certainly wasn't his seniority that allowed him to stay. Amanda figured it was the quality of his work. He wasn't the most dedicated member of the crew, but when he put his mind to it, he did amazing work. Amanda always felt a mentor-ish bond between Jeff and Andrew. Jeff treated Andrew like the son he never had and Andrew treated Jeff like the father he never wanted. Jeff would attempt to mentor Andrew and Andrew would always rebel and push away only to come back and accept the help a short time later. It was a dysfunctional relationship, but it worked.

The fifth and final member of their crew today didn't get to keep his position because of skill, Amanda was sure of that. Simon had been around for at least 15 years. Amanda wasn't sure exactly when he was hired, or how he even managed to get hired. He too must have been hired directly out of high school, because Amanda guessed he was no more than 35 years old. His facial features had softened a little over the years, but his attitude and demeanor hadn't.

Simon was easily the least liked member of the crew. He was harsh, abrasive, and never shy about telling you exactly what he was thinking. In a small way, which she would never admit aloud, she admired him for speaking his mind. In a large way, which she also would never admit aloud, she hated just about everything else about him. The way he spoke down to everyone, his superiority complex, the way he chewed his food.

Normally, Amanda would never hate anyone, but getting to know Simon meant hating him. Even after a decade of working with him, she never noticed him making a single friend. He came to work, bitched a lot, and went home. That was Simon's function. Even after all the issues Jeff had had with Simon over the years, Amanda figured his seniority kept him around.

She was reminded of several times when Simon's arrogance caused injuries to the crew. There was the scar on Kyle's ear that Simon had caused during the worse incident that Amanda had ever seen. Once, Simon wasn't looking where he was swinging a sledgehammer and broke two fingers on the hand of a female crew member. Also, there was the time when Simon was using a wood router near Andrew, which resulted in Andrew getting a splinter in his eye. The thought of any of the injuries made Amanda shutter.

Amanda looked Simon up and down. He was wearing a light weight jacket and the same boots she had seen him in every day for the past several years. His hair matched Jeff's and shined with strands of white, in sharp contrast to his natural black. He had stone cold brown eyes and Amanda hated looking into them. She wasn't sure if it was fear she would see or simply desperation, but even looking into his eyes made Amanda uncomfortable.

She turned her focus to Jeff who was going over the intake paperwork that Sandy had prepared on her final day with the company. Jeff fumbled with papers as they threatened to blow away in the frigid breeze. He found the one he was looking for and secured it with his right hand while managing to tuck the rest under his arm.

"Okay, Sandy said we need five guys," he said, looking around counting. "This is a simple gutting job. In 3 weeks this entire building is schedule to be turned into a spa resort and--"

Simon cut him off. "A spa resort? In New Castle, Pennsylvania? Since when is this shit hole a resort town?"

Jeff continued, "We need to completely gut the inside so they can begin the renovation." He pulled a set of keys out of his pocket and walked over to the front door. There were 3 keys on the ring. He tried the first one but it did not unlock. He put the second one in and it turned with ease. Jeff pushed open the door and entered the building. The rest of the crew followed. They were in a small lobby area.

The entire lobby was maybe the size of a small dorm room. They were all able to crowd in. The temperate didn't seem to rise, but it did protect them from the wind. A single light bulb burned above their heads, providing only the minimum amount of light needed to see.

Jeff was only a few steps from them and already at the far side of the lobby. Here, there was another set of doors. This was a set of double doors made of wrought iron bars. It was too dark to see much inside of them, but Amanda noticed the tops of them were spear shaped. She wondered how sharp the tops were. They came to a very fine point. It almost seemed out of place to have a gate like this inside a building. Amanda guessed it was a purely aesthetic choice since the front door was obviously meant to keep out intruders.

Jeff took the key ring again and fumbled around until he found the key to the gates. As Jeff unlatched the door, the sound echoed inside the mausoleum. Amanda's imagination ran wild with what they would find when they finally entered the place. Would there be dead bodies still around for them to remove? Surely that wouldn't be legal, right?

Jeff pushed open the double gates. They screeched to life with a roar that nearly vibrated the floor the crew was standing on. The musty air poured in from the mausoleum. The iron gates were easy to see through, but it was almost as if there was an invisible shield keeping the smell out of the lobby. The crew passed through the iron gates one by one until each one of them was standing just inside the massive mausoleum.

Amanda tried to look around but the only

light was coming from the dim bulb in the lobby. Someone had closed the front door to keep out the chilling breeze and Amanda squinted to see the room in front of her. Her eyes slowly began to adjust to the low light and she began to get flashes of the room in front of her. White Marble. Gold plated grave markers. Piles of smashed tiles and marble.

A loud humming sound filled Amanda's ears and harsh florescent light began to fill the room. Jeff had found the breaker box and flipped the switch. At first this made it harder for the crew to see. Kyle and Amanda put their hands over their eyes and Andrew looked down at the ground.

A thick layer of dust covered the breaker box, which led Jeff to dust off his hands as he rejoined the group. The dust formed a cloud above their heads, and as soon as it began to settle, everyone got a good look at the room in front of them.

They were in the very front of the mausoleum. The mausoleum was divided into two halves. Each half was made up of one long, straight hallway that ran all the way to the back of the mausoleum. Each hallway was lined floor to ceiling, on both sides, with burial chambers. They were stacked 8 high and as long as they eye could see. The building was built to hold hundreds of resting souls.

Jeff looked down again at his paperwork

and began to walk down one of the hallways. Amanda and Andrew followed closely behind. Lyle and Kyle walked together, in unison, and Simon lurked behind.

"The structure is made up of two parallel hallways," Jeff said in his most authoritative voice. "The structure was built in 1923 and at its peak held over 2,000 caskets."

A voice spoke up from the back of the tour, "I feel like I'm at a fucking museum. Just tell me what the hell we are doing here," Simon said.

Jeff ignored him and kept speaking. "The doors on the burial chambers are one inch thick marble. The entire building is not made of marble, but there is a one inch thick layer of it covering virtually the entire inside." Andrew reached out and knocked on the wall between two burial chambers. It felt pretty solid to him.

"They are scheduled to begin construction in the spring on a luxury resort and spa and they've contracted us to remove the insides of the place. They want nothing but 4 walls when they start."

Kyle spoke up, "They are building a luxury resort? Here? In the middle of nowhere?" Jeff ignored this comment as well.

"Are all of these tombs empty?" Andrew asked.

"Yes," Jeff replied. "Although some may still contain caskets, all of the bodies have been moved to a final resting place."

Those words sent a chill running down Andrew's spine. Final Resting Place. Everything about this place felt final.

Andrew turned around to see what the rest of the crew was doing behind him. Lyle and Kyle had both taken to trying to open the burial chambers. A few were sealed tight. Kyle had managed to crack one open and peek inside, but the marble was not willing to move from its final resting place. Andrew got a feeling that this was not going to be an easy job.

Before he even realized it, they were at the far end of the mausoleum. The back wall of the structure was completely bare except for a single door. Andrew realized that if there was a hallway down the center, there would be a door at each end.

Jeff reached for the doorknob and opened the small wooden door. There was no sign on the outside to give even the slightest clue as to what might be behind it. Jeff entered first and fumbled around looking for a light switch. When he finally did find it, it barely illuminated the room. It reminded Amanda of being back in the lobby. A single dim bulb and it hurt her eyes to readjust to the darkness.

One by one the crew entered the small room and as their eyes readjusted to the dark they realized it was an office. There was a desk with an antique phone, a bookshelf that had long since been relieved of its duties, and a calendar on the wall that read 1979.

While Jeff tried to find his place in his notes, Amanda and Andrew looked around. The floor in this room felt different than outside in the burial area. The forgiving wood floors in here were a sharp contrast to the unforgiving marble outside. Andrew walked over to the far side of the room and noticed the floor almost had a bounce to it.

There was a door on the back wall of the office. Andrew cracked it open and peeked inside. It was a small bathroom that looked like it hadn't been touched since the 70's. The walls were a pale pink and green tile and the fixtures had long since rusted. There was still a drop of water dripping from the faucet and sliding effortlessly down the rusted drain.

Simon was standing at the wall that ran perpendicular to the left of the bathroom. The wall had several old document holders hanging on it. They were all empty with shattered glass. One held a spider's web, but the spider appeared long gone.

There was door on the wall. Simon tried the door knob, but it was locked. He shook it and dust fell from the hinges. It appeared to be firmly locked.

Amanda was near the wall that ran perpendicular to the right of the bathroom. It was made of wood planks and almost seemed like an after thought. The rest of the room was once painted, although now most of it had peeled off and rested on the wood floor. The planks appeared to be cedar and Amanda noticed their imperfections almost immediately. They were curved and splintered in all the wrong places. The nails holding them up had long since rusted and each board held a wealth of knots and holes.

Andrew joined Amanda near the wall and attempted to look through several of the holes. It was no use. The lone light bulb that dangled from the ceiling was barely enough to light the office, let alone provide enough light to clue him in on what may have been hiding behind the wall.

Amanda locked eyes with Andrew for just a moment. It was long enough for her to realize they were both thinking the same thing. Why had this wall been so hastily put up? Before they could investigate any further, Jeff found his place in his notes.

"This was the caretaker's office. We have been instructed not to touch this. We only need to worry about removing the marble facing and burial tomb doors."

"So why are we in here then?" Simon asked.

Jeff took notice this time he spoke. "Good question. Everybody out," he instructed. "Go get your tools and I will meet you back near the front door in 5 minutes."

The crew left the office, single file, back into the cold reality of the burial area. Jeff allowed the crew to exit and reached for the light. He turned around to allow himself one last look at the office. The flipped the switch and darkness engulfed the room. He pulled the door closed behind him never noticing the eye that was watching them from behind the cedar plank wall.

5

Sandy looked down at the clock on the dashboard. 7:27. She quickly finished getting ready after discovering it was a simple popped breaker that caused he earlier scare. She didn't even take the time to warm up the car and she was already off and running for the day. She had things to do and wasn't going to let her mood get the best of her.

She glanced from the dashboard up to the small building sitting in front of her. The front was lined with spotless glass that betrayed the dingy sign hanging in the window. It read: Hardy Flowers.

Sandy had been coming here for years. Every time she needed a pick-me-up should would stop by and pick up some fresh flowers. She would spend hours at night arranging them and strategically placing them around the house. She loved the small amount of control it brought her. She would place one or two in a vase just to get an idea of what she wanted. If she didn't like the color or the texture of the chosen flowers, she would pull them all out and start over again.

She would try many different combinations. She loved playing around with colors and smells. Sometimes, she would find it very difficult. Even though she built one she loved, she still wanted to tear it down and start all over again. Sandy loved creating the structure of the arrangements.

Today, she thought she might try something different. She wanted to ask Scott, the flower store manager, what was in season. She squinted to see if she could make out anything in the coolers just inside the front door, but the clouds in the sky blocked the light and all she could see was the reflection of her car.

Sandy looked down at the clock again. 7:30 exactly. Scott should be opening the store soon. Sure enough, just as she thought it, Scott unlocked the front door. She saw him and flashed him a big smile. He seemed to notice her but didn't smile back. Sandy was taken aback for a minute. He was always happy to see her. They had spent countless hours over the past decade chatting about flowers. She had even brought in arrangements for his approval over the years and he always willingly shared tips, and his opinion, with her.

Not waiting another second to find out why she wasn't warmly greeted, Sandy turned off the ignition and hopped out into the cold frigid air. She was dressed in her warmest coat, scarf, and gloves, but the wind still pushed through and chilled her skin. She hit the automatic lock on the car and ran to the front door of the flower shop.

She pulled open the door and felt as if she had just stepped off of a plane in Bermuda. The hot and sticky air made her lungs feel heavy. As her eyes readjusted to the light inside the flower shop, she noticed why Scott had not given her a smile. It had nothing to do with her.

Sandy found Scott standing behind the counter looking. She walked over to him and asked, "What happened?"

"They're all dead," Scott said with a tremble in his voice.

"It's terrible. How did this happen?"

"There was a malfunction with the furnace. It tripped a breaker, the refrigerators lost power, and the heat ran all night." Scott said.

They were dead. Every single flower in the store was dead. Sandy took a closer look around from her view point at the counter. The arrangements directly behind Scott's head were wilted with leaves and petals still regularly falling to the ground. The coolers that lined the back of the store reminded Sandy of a tomb for flowers. Behind each glass door was soft brown death.

Sandy walked along the length of the coolers. Each one held more horror than the next.

It was January. It was supposed to be a new beginning. A chance at a fresh start. Sandy was counting on that fresh start. The flowers that were so green and colorful were now deeply brown and lifeless.

Sandy passed cooler after cooler of loss. Not even a single salvageable flower. Sandy thought about what it was like to be one of those flowers, trapped behind an invisible wall and unable to escape to save your life. Slowly suffocating with no chance of survival. Gasping for air in the final moments.

She had to clear her mind. She was overacting again. They were just flowers. Surely Scott would order new ones and they would be here in a day or two. She looked away from that final cooler and took a deep breath to bring her back to reality.

"Scott, this is just so awful. It makes me angry. All of those beautiful flowers. Gone," she said.

"I have to call the repairman today and see if I can get any delivery men to come ASAP. I'm sorry I don't have anything for you this morning," Scott said apologetic.

"It's okay," Sandy understood. "I will just have to go somewhere else for my flowers today." Sandy regretted saying that almost as soon as it came out of her mouth. On a normal day Scott would just quip right back at her. But she wasn't sure how much of an impact losing all of his inventory would have on him.

"I hear K-Mart does great work," he deadpanned.

Sandy let out a chuckle for the first time today.

"What the hell," she said back to him. "It can't get any worse than this!"

6

Lyle dropped the tailgate on his truck. He hopped up in the bed and slid a toolbox the length of bed to Kyle. Kyle opened the box, pulled out a worn brown leather tool belt, and began to stock it with tools from the shiny metallic box. Lyle opened a dull metallic box, pulled out a new brown leather belt, and began to do the same.

They both instinctively knew what they would need for a demo job and started pulling tools from their boxes and equipping their belts.

Kyle reached into the box and pulled out a small hammer. As he slid it into the belt, he noticed a large spot of rust on the tailgate of the pickup.

"I don't know how you can continue to drive this piece of junk," he said to his brother.

"What are you talking about? This thing is a classic," Lyle said, 100% believing the words as they came out of his mouth.

"A classic? You've had it since high school. I think the word you're looking for is--"

Lyle cut him off. "Hey, this thing got me laid 3 times a week in high school. There's no way I'm giving up this good luck charm."

"Yeah," Kyle said, "But what has it done for you lately?"

Lyle withdrew a package of steel wool from the toolbox and gave it a playful chuck directly as his brother's head. Kyle easily batted it off and it fell to the ground. He reached down and picked it up and stuffed it in his tool belt.

"Thanks, I needed that."

Kyle finished stuffing his belt full of tools and slid the box back down the bed of the pickup truck to his brother. Lyle was already finished and tightening his belt when his brother's toolbox slid to a stop at his feet.

Lyle slid them both into the corner of the truck bed, and retreated back towards his brother, who had already slammed the tailgate shut. Lyle hopped over the corner of the truck and the brothers walked back to the front of the mausoleum.

As they walked through the front door, Kyle looked over his shoulder and saw Amanda and Andrew over by her car, Jeff near his, but no sign of Simon. Kyle figured he must be back inside already.

Kyle walked through the front door, past the iron gates, and into the mausoleum. He waited a minute for his eyes to adjust and looked around for his brother and Simon. He didn't see either.

He walked a few paces to the right and looked down the eastern hallway. He could see all the way to the end of the hallway and there was no one there. He walked back to the other side of the mausoleum and looked down the western hallway. They had to be down there. There really was no place to hide in this large old building. The design didn't allow for it. He looked down the hallway; empty.

Kyle wondered were they could be. He walked back to the center of the mausoleum and looked through the iron gates into the lobby area. It was dimly lit but he could see the entire area. It was also deserted.

For a moment, Kyle considered panicking. Lyle had walked through these doors no more than 10 seconds before he had, where could he have possibly gone? But, then he remembered who he was dealing with. Lyle loved to be the center of attention and was always pulling jokes on people.

There was a time, in high school, when they both thought the same way. They were always messing around with their buddies, trying to scare their girlfriends, or pulling some juvenile prank on their parents. But, soon after graduation, they both found out high school was as good as it was going to get for both of them.

The fun times and jokes they had played at 17 didn't seem to go over so well at 20. They began spending less time together and attempted to forge their own identities.

New Castle was as small town and they soon found out that nearly everyone they knew always thought about them as a pair. They wanted to be thought of as individuals. First Lyle died his hair and began working out at the gym. Kyle cut his hair short and began making new friends through work. It wasn't until they both landed a job at Crane Construction that they both started to hang out regularly again. Ever since then they became inseparable again.

They both felt those few years in young adulthood allowed them to enough time to forge their own identities that they were distinguishable as individuals.

Kyle took a deep breath and turned to face the rows of burial chambers again. Lyle was hiding out somewhere in here and he was going to beat him at his own game.

He walked to the right and paced down the eastern hallway. He looked up and down at the hundreds of burial chambers. They were both trying to open them earlier, but they wouldn't budge. He wouldn't be hiding in one of those.

Kyle had made it no more than 2 burial chambers deep that the next 3 chambers appeared to have their marble loosened. That wasn't like that before. What if this wasn't Lyle playing a prank on him? What if this was something else? The entire building gave him an odd feeling. A feeling he hadn't had since their grandmother's funeral when they were kids.

He approached the first burial chamber. He kicked the marble and it fell loose and slammed to the ground. The loud sound of marble crashing on marble, even from such a short distance was almost deafening. It echoed throughout the entire mausoleum and came back around seconds later to hit him one more time.

Kyle bent over to get a better look inside the tomb. He couldn't see anything. The marble falling had formed a cloud of dust that lingered inside the chamber. He reached into this tool belt and pulled out his flashlight. He aimed it directly into the tomb and clicked it to life. He prepared himself for a shock. A dead body. His brother jumping out to scare him. At the bare minimum a rat. But there was nothing. The light reflected back at him. Kyle could see the end of the chamber. It was about 7 feet deep and maybe 3 feet high, and it was bare.

He took a deep breath trying to avoid the dust and moved along to the next burial chamber. This time, he was careful to avoid even tapping it for fear of it falling over.

Kyle pulled a pair of gloves out of his tool belt and slid them on. After all of these years in the business, it was habit to put on gloves before doing any heavy lifting.

He reached for the marble slab cover and gripped it firmly with two hands from the top. At first the slab had no give, but Kyle worked it back and forth, left to right, until it began to loosen. Once he felt the initial movement it fell off quickly and he placed it delicately on the ground. The slab wasn't nearly as heavy as he was expecting it to be, considering it was pure marble. Maybe this job wasn't going to be as bad as he thought.

Kyle took the flashlight back out of his belt and prepared himself again for the jump scare. He clicked the flashlight and illuminated the tomb: empty.

This brought a smile to Kyle's face. He was about to beat his brother at his own game. It was a simple process of elimination. Lyle was hiding in the third chamber. Kyle thought about his moves for a second and decided he knew exactly how to play it.

Kyle stood directly next to the tomb with his back against the burial chambers. He mentally prepared himself for the noise again and gave the marble slab a quick hard kick. It loosened easily and fell to the ground. The sound was somewhat softer this time, perhaps because Kyle knew what to expect.

He waited next to the chamber. If Lyle was hiding in there, Kyle was not going to give him the satisfaction of jumping out and scaring him. Kyle didn't realize that he was holding his breath. He didn't want to make a sound to alert his brother that he was standing right outside of his hiding place. He figured Lyle would just think the marble wasn't put back on correctly and just fell off.

But nothing happened.

Patience wasn't a virtue that either of the Harper brothers were blessed with. Now it would simply become a game of chicken as to who could hold out longer. Kyle would be the first to admit that he usually lost this game.

Still nothing happened.

The time started to add up in Kyle's mind. How long had he been standing here waiting for Lyle to pop his head out and ruin the surprise? Surely it had only been seconds, but it began to feel like minutes. As Kyle allowed himself a single breath, the minutes turned into hours and he gave up. He jumped in front of the tomb and gave his brother the opportunity to have some fun.

But nothing happened.

Lyle didn't jump out. Kyle clicked his flashlight to life once again and shined it directly into the tomb. This one was different then the last two. The light didn't reflect back at him like it did in the empty chambers. That's when Kyle realized that the chamber wasn't empty. It was filled with something, and it wasn't his brother. It was a casket.

Kyle was immediately taken back to his grandmother's funeral again. The shiny brown wood was polished so much that you could practically see yourself in the refection. It was dead quiet in the funeral home that day and their parents forced Lyle and Kyle to sit near the back and be on their best behavior.

The silence, the shiny brown wood, the smell of death in the air forced Kyle to face mortality. If his brother wasn't hiding in this tomb, where was he? Had something happened to him?

Kyle noticed for the first time that the casket appeared to be on some sort of track. He used the flashlight to illuminate it and saw a handle on the end of the coffin. He reached out and grabbed it. The cold metal made the hair on his arm stand on end. He gave it a quick pull to see if it would move and it easily did. Only using a small amount of his strength Kyle had pulled the casket nearly halfway out of the tomb.

He pulled a little harder and it was fully out. Kyle wondered why it was so easy to pull out. Was there often a need to move the caskets in and out? Didn't Jeff say all of the bodies had been moved to a final resting place?

Something happened.

Kyle wasn't exactly sure what it was, but he was sure he heard some kind of movement from inside the casket. He looked around for some kind of latch but the casket was already ajar. The shiny brown lid was just asking to be opened.

He reached down and grabbed the cover of the casket. He once again held his breath as he slowly began to open it. He could see the shiny brown exterior meet the plush ivory of the lining. The ripples and the folds seemed to melt into each other and grow deeper and deeper into the casket.

There was a loud cracking noise and the cover stopped moving. Kyle nearly jumped out of his skin as his eyes focused trying to make sense of what was happening. He let out a hard breath when he realized the top cover of the casket had hit the top of the burial chamber. He hadn't pulled it out far enough.

At this point Kyle was exasperated at the entire situation. He grab the casket from the handle, gave it a quick hard jolt to ensure it was clear of the tomb and flipped open the cover.

His scream echoed throughout the entire mausoleum and traveled out the front door.

7

Amanda threw open the trunk of her car. This was as close as she came to anger.

"Again? You really didn't bring any tools?" She said to Andrew, who was standing next to her trying his best to throw his charming smile.

"I walked here. I would have never made it on time with all of those tools dragging me down," he tried to rationalize to her. She didn't really buy it, he always knew he could count on good old over prepared Amanda to cover for him.

"I'm not buying that for a second," she barked. Andrew believed her. He never expected her to buy into what he was saying, he just expected her to help him out.

"Please? I promise it will never happen again," he said with a childish grin on his face.

"I believe that's the 172nd time I've heard that," she said. Her anger began to fade when she looked into his bright blue eyes, but she tried her best not to show it. "You do realized that you shouldn't even be here, right?"

That comment brought Andrew back down from his puppy dog smile high.

She continued, "It's only because Jeff can't interpret his own notes that he hasn't even noticed yet."

"Why did you even do it if you're just going to constantly bring it up?"

She thought about it for a minute. She knew exactly what he meant. Her cold exterior began to fade and she let the real Amanda begin to shine through again.

"I'm sorry, I'm sorry. Here take my old belt," she said reaching into the trunk and producing a rugged looking black tool belt.

Andrew grinned again and strapped it around his waist. He was surprised that he and Amanda both wore it on the same belt notch, but thought better of sharing that thought out loud.

"But," Amanda said, "I need some insurance."

"Excuse me?"

"Do you know how many tools I've lost to you over the years?" Andrew couldn't tell if she was being serious, or playful.

"None," he snarked back at her.

"Your phone," she said looking cold into his eyes.

"What about it?"

"Give it to me." Amanda held out her hand.

Andrew bit his lip and considered the alternative. No tools, no work. He reached into his pocket and pulled out his phone. He slapped it down in Amanda's hand.

"You know how Jeff feels about phones on a job site anyway. We'll leave them both here and when you give back the tools, you can have your phone back."

Amanda reached into her pocket and gathered her phone. She checked it for any messages and gently placed both of them in the trunk. She was just about to reach for her tool belt when they heard a scream coming from inside the mausoleum.

***

Jeff was standing near his car when it happened. He meant to get his tools, but he got distracted by his cell phone ringing. By the time he got it out of the leather holder around his waist, it was a missed call.

He scrolled through the call history to find out who it was from. By the time he got to the correct screen, a voicemail had come through and he figured it was just easier to listen to the voicemail.

Jeff was not very good with technology. Many of the other construction companies that had moved into town used tablet computers to keep track of notes and blue prints, but not Jeff Crane. He still used the same paper and clipboard based system that Sandy had put into effect decades ago. He wasn't about to go changing things now. He needed some stability in his life. Now that Sandy was gone, nothing about his business, the one that they had virtually built together, seemed familiar. By hanging on to her paperwork system, he was able to feel like everything wasn't spiraling out of control.

He tapped the number one on the hasn't-been-updated-since-they-were-invented cell phone and put it to his ear. It was a call about another job. He didn't even get to hear what the job was before a scream came through the frigid air and pierced Jeff's ear.

***

Simon was hiding behind the row of burial chambers. The ends of both rows provided the only shelter without crawling into a tomb itself. He wasn't about to do that.

He felt like he was the only one around who ever did any work. That bitch Amanda was everyone's favorite, but he could see right through her. She claimed she worked hard but she really just sucked everyone's dick to get to where she was today. She was always up Jeff's ass and the first one to be in line for any shitty job he offered.

Simon was already inside with his tools and Amanda was still out there talking to that jerk off Andrew. If there was one person Simon couldn't stand, it was him. He walked through life with a smile and that ridiculous long hair and figured just by displaying some charm he can weasel his way into (or out of) anything.

That was pretty much all Simon had to say about Andrew: the weasel.

The brothers were okay. He had a few fun jobs with them over the years, but they weren't always on the same page. Simon still had a scar on his wrist from where Kyle and he got into a fight.

That was part of the reason today why he decided to help Lyle scare the shit out of his brother.

Simon was jerked back out of his thoughts by the sound of a second large crashing through the mausoleum. He carefully peered from behind the row of burial chambers and saw Kyle standing next to an open tomb. Simon figured he must have figured out the game and was attempting to search for his brother.

He knew that wasn't going to happen. Simon hid back behind the row of chambers and waited. He heard the casket rolling out. The casket lid opening and Kyle screaming for his life. That's when Simon jumped out from behind the chambers and made a made dash for Kyle.

8

Kyle stared down at his brother Lyle lying in the casket. He couldn't believe he actually fell for another one of Lyle's tricks. Lyle had jumped up at him as soon as Kyle had opened the lid. Kyle let out a terrified shriek and Lyle knew his brother was scared out of his mind. Now, Lyle laid in the casket, clutching his stomach, trying to catch his breath.

Before Kyle even had a chance to react, Simon was standing behind him, doubled over laughing with Lyle.

Kyle turned to face him, "you were in on this, asshole?"

Simon wiped a tear from his face and chuckled back at Kyle, "how the hell else do you think he got in there?"

By the time Kyle turned around to face Lyle again, the rest of the gang had arrived, no doubt responding to his scream.

Amanda, Andrew, and Jeff stood in front of him and immediately knew they had also been the victim of Lyle and Simon's prank. They weren't quite sure what the prank was, and the truth was, they were so used to Lyle and Kyle's joking, that it didn't register to any of them to ask what had happened.

Kyle bent over and looked his brother directly in the face. "You are an asshole," he said, and slammed the casket lid shut. Lyle was still laughing inside. Kyle attempted to storm out, but only made it two steps before something stopped him.

For a nanosecond, it felt as if it was an earthquake. But, that was only the beginning. Simultaneously the floor began to shake, and marble began to fall off of the burial chambers. Dust filled the room as the walls around them began to crumble.

None of the crew had a chance to take cover. They all stood helplessly as the room began to crash down around them. They didn't know it at the time, but the collapse that shook the floor and brought down the walls also sealed them inside the mausoleum.

9

Jeff was the first one to open his eyes. The collapse happened so suddenly that no one had any time to react. Jeff was laying on the ground in the fetal position. There was debris all over him. He attempted to open his eyes, but the thick layer of marble dust that danced in the air did not allow him to see more than a foot in front of him.

He screamed instead, "Is everyone okay?"

There was no response. He immediately

began to panic and brushed the marble pieces and rotted wood from inside the burial tombs off of him. He felt around his body for any injuries. Everything felt intact and he attempted to stand up. Jeff made it up to his feet but breathing in the dust made him feel light headed and he had to hold on to a pile of rubble for balance.

He coughed as the dust filled his lungs. It burned and Jeff could feel it bonding to his insides. He pulled his shirt up and placed it over his nose and mouth in an attempt to find some clean air. The dust began to dissipate and Jeff was thankful to notice that most of the lighting throughout the mausoleum was still on.

Jeff squinted to make out any detail in the ruins around him. He could still vaguely see that the building had not collapsed. The lighting at the far end of the mausoleum was still on and Jeff could see all the way to the end. He turned around to look behind him. It appeared that the row of burial chambers had come crashing down. Jeff could see through the pile of fallen marble the second row of burial chambers on the west side of the mausoleum. They were still standing.

The front door was completely blocked. The collapse seemed to have taken aim at the entrance. The marble had collapsed and completely filled the small lobby area and formed a mountain outside where the iron gates had been. The gates, Jeff thought. He couldn't even see them. They must have been buried beneath the debris.

Looking up, Jeff could see the roof was intact. It was just the row of burial chambers. The thought did cross his mind that this would make their job easier, since that was one of the tasks they were assigned to complete in the demo. Jeff was quickly brought back to reality when he heard the sound of moaning.

"Hello,' he called out, to no one in particular.

"What happened?" He heard a voice call back to him.

"Simon, is that you?" Jeff immediately recognized his voice.

"Yeah," Simon responded.

Jeff squinted in an attempt to see Simon in front of him.

"I think the row of burial chambers gave out and collapsed. Can you see anyone else?" Just as Jeff had asked the question, he made out the outline of Simon's muscular body hulking towards him. He didn't appear to be seriously injured. He was upright and mobile. Jeff wasn't worried about Simon. He was the toughest member of the crew. Simon had been through much more than a partial building collapse.

Simon was far enough away from the epicenter that he wasn't injured. His immediate instinct was to jump up and run, but his head wouldn't allow it. He laid low on the ground until he grew accustomed to breathing in the dust. He finally stood when he could see and was walking toward the sound of Jeff's voice when he tripped over something.

He went down hard, nearly hitting his head on a nearby broken marble slab.

"Shit," he screamed as he hit the ground.

"Simon, what happened? Are you okay?" Jeff had lost sight of him.

"I fell over--"

Before Simon could finish his sentence, he realized that he hadn't tripped over rubble. He tripped over a body.

"Oh, shit," he said again. It was one of the few words in his limited vocabulary.

He felt around on the ground. The body was partially buried with marble. Simon began unbury the body. He pulled off marble and wood, being as careful as he can to avoid stabbing himself with the splintered wood pieces.

The dust continued to lift and Simon was finally able to get a better look at what he was doing. He would recognize that bright orange coat anywhere. It was Kyle. He was partially buried in the marble remains. Simon worked harder and faster to unbury him. He threw small and medium sized pieces of marble behind him, hitting the external wall of the mausoleum. He pulled larger sized pieces and pushed them as far away from Kyle as he could.

Several pieces of wood began to snag his shirt and several large wood splinters stabbed through the soft flannel of his shirt and pierced his skin. Soon his shirt was moist with warm blood. Simon moved a large piece of marble and revealed Kyle's head. He was unconscious. But, was he dead?

Simon thought to reach for his neck to find a pulse, but an arm had already come from behind his head to do the same thing. Simon looked up to find Jeff standing over him, with his hand on Kyle's neck.

"He's alive," Jeff said. Together, they scanned Kyle's body for any major injuries, but he appeared to be undamaged.

Kyle's head began to rock from side to side and his eyes slowly opened.

"Kyle," Jeff said. "There was a partial building collapse. Are you all right?"

Simon wondered how Jeff could be back to all business so soon after the incident. The tone to his voice was cold and professional. The exact same tone he had only a half hour ago when he was showing them around the building.

Kyle took his right hand and felt around his body. He started with his head and moved down from there.

"It doesn't look like you have any major injuries," Jeff said to him, not knowing if Kyle was understanding a word he said.

"I," Kyle paused, "think. I'm alright."

His voice was shaky but he attempted to sit up. He put his hand on his head as he did and closed his eyes. He opened them again to a startling vision standing right behind Simon and Jeff. Kyle pointed his finger up and said, "is that a ghost?"

Jeff and Simon turned to find Amanda standing behind them. She was in a daze. Blood flowed from an open wound on her head and dripped off of her ear onto her shoulder. She stared at Kyle but he had no idea if she understood what was going on.

"Amanda?" Jeff said, standing to face her.

Hearing her name brought her out of her daze. She made eye contact with Jeff and noticed Simon standing next to him, and Kyle staggering to his feet behind them.

"What happened?" she said.

"There was a partial collapse," business Jeff was back. He spoke even slower to Amanda.

Her eyes were still blank, although she was responsive. She seemed unaware of the gash in her skull.

"You're bleeding," Simon said.

Amanda reached up and touched her head. Pain filled her body and blinded her sight. She pulled her hand down and saw it covered with blood. She wasn't the squeamish type, but seeing her hand return to her cover in red sticky death, made her lose all of her energy.

She struggled to stay standing and Jeff grabbed her arm to balance her. "I need to you to stay strong Amanda," he said to her. He walked around behind her, still firmly grasping her arm, and inspected the wound the best he could in the dim florescent light.

Even though it didn't look too bad, he downplayed it to Amanda. "It's not bad at all. It's already stopped bleeding. Here," he said. He pulled one of his layered shirts off and gave it to Amanda. She held it against her head and took a closer look around the room. She didn't see Andrew. He was standing right next to her with the collapse happened.

"Where's Andrew?" she asked with a panic in her voice.

The dust had dissipated enough for the crew to get a much better look at their surroundings. The partial collapse of one of the 2 rows of burial chambers had cornered them off near the front of the mausoleum. The front door was completely blocked and the iron gates that seemed so out of place seemed to have disappeared into the rubble. The other row of burial chambers seemed intact and only about a quarter of the row nearest them had collapsed. There was still plenty more in this building that could come down.

Jeff was the first to notice Andrew's legs sticking out of the marble wreckage. Jeff expected him to look like the wicked witch with a house on top of him, but he didn't look anything like that. He was sticking out of the marble at an unnatural angle. He legs were both crossed and facing the outside wall of the mausoleum. There was no blood but everything from Andrew's waist up was buried in rubble.

For the first time since the collapse, the crew became aware of the sounds around them. All of their ears were still ringing but they began to get back bits and pieces of natural sound. Jeff picked out some marble settling. Amanda noticed the hum from the florescent lights high about them on the ceiling. Kyle noticed a faint but rhythmic thumping sound he also assumed was coming from the lights.

The crew rushed over to Andrew and began frantically trying to clear him from the rubble. Blood dripped from Simon's arms onto the marble, making it difficult for him to grab the sleek, heavy slabs.

Amanda threw Jeff's shirt down to the ground and began to dig through the ruins. For the first time, the entire team was working as a cohesive unit. Deep down inside it gave Amanda a sense of accomplishment. This was the team she had spent so many years with.

It seemed like seconds and the team had started to uncover Andrew. First his right arm, uninjured to the naked eye. Next was his torso. It was like putting together a jigsaw puzzle.

Andrew's left arm was pinned behind his back, a victim of the strange angle at which he was trapped.

As the crew uncovered the next piece of the demented jigsaw puzzle, they saw why Andrew was laying at such an unnatural angle. He was laying on top of the collapsed iron gates. One of the spear shaped rods had made its way through his shoulder and rested on a slab of shiny red marble.

Jeff pulled back the marble and handed it to Simon. Simon grabbed at it, but the amount of blood on it made it slippery and it crashed to the floor. The sound jerked Andrew to life and he began to scream.

He was virtually free from the collapsed marble now, but the spear through his back, exiting his shoulder, kept him pinned to the ground. He screamed again when he tried to stand, and Amanda dropped down to her knees to be by his side.

She rested her hand on his head but it did not stop his screaming.

"Shut up, that's not helping," screamed Simon in his general direction.

Jeff also dropped to his knees on the other side of Andrew. Andrew met his eyes but the pain in his shoulder wouldn't subside. He couldn't stop screaming.

Amanda looked at Jeff, "we have to do something, he's pinned here in pain."

Jeff looked around searching for something. "Tools?" he asked to no one in particular.

He, Amanda, and Andrew ran in without their tool belts when Kyle screamed. Simon didn't bring his either, he was too busy helping Lyle execute his prank. The group turned to Kyle who was still wearing his tool belt. Jeff surveyed Kyle's waist to see if there was anything that could help. Kyle was wearing a hammer on one side, and a matching hatchet on the other side. There was a flashlight and a variety of screwdrivers, but nothing that was going to help calm Andrew's pain.

Andrew screamed again and the rhythmic pounding in Kyle's ears began to fade into the background.

"Shut up," Simon said. He tried covering his ears but it was no use. Andrew's uncontrollable screams were unavoidable. It was beginning to get to Simon.

"Do you think we should try to move him?" Amanda asked, turning her attention back to Jeff.

"I don't think we can, he's pinned down."

Andrew screamed again. Sweat ran down his forehead and neck onto his shoulder. The salty sting only agitated the wound.

"We have to try something, he's in agony," Amanda reasoned.

"All right," Jeff said. "What about trying

to hack off the end of the spike with the hatchet?"

It was a ludicrous suggestion. Amanda wasn't thinking clearly after her head injury, but even she knew it was ludicrous.

"Will somebody shut him the fuck up," Simon said. He began pacing behind the group and was clearly losing his cool.

Amanda turned to Andrew. She grabbed his head and forced him to focus on her.

"Andrew, we are going to help you, but I need to you to calm down. I know it hurts but the only way we are going to get you out of here is if you stay calm," Amanda said in her calmest tone.

It seemed to work. Andrew stopped screaming. His breathing was heavy and sweat ran from his forehead in all angles.

Kyle watched as Amanda calmed Andrew down. The rhythmic thumping once again started in his head as soon as Andrew stopped screaming.

"That's better. I know it hurts, but--"

Jeff attempted to place his hand on Andrew's leg, but inadvertently moved a piece of the fallen marble. It started a chain reaction and a small chuck of wood fell from the debris pile and landed on Andrew's injured shoulder. The pain was unbearable and he began to scream again.

The newest scream sent Simon over the

edge. He let out a scream of his own and pushed by Amanda and Jeff. The slightest push knocked Amanda over and she fell on top of a small pile of marble shards.

Simon grabbed Andrew by both shoulders and Andrew let out another agonizing scream of pain. Simon pulled with all of his might, determined no matter what damage, to get Andrew up and to stop his horrific screams.

The spike in Andrew's right shoulder began to move as his head flopped forward. It inched backwards out of his body tearing whatever was in its way. Andrew could feel ligaments tearing as the spike struck a bone on the way out. The spike was nearly out when Simon lost his grip. His hands were bloody and sweaty and he couldn't properly grip Andrew's shoulders.

Andrew let out another ghastly yelp as the spike drove another hole into his shoulder. The rest of the crew looked on in horror. They wanted Andrew to stop yelling as much as Simon did, but none of them had the guts to do anything about it. Amanda wanted to stop him, but her body was frozen in horror at the action unfolding in front of her.

Simon was undeterred. He grabbed Andrew by the shoulders again, and this time pulled harder. With one final scraping of the bone the Andrew was pulled off of the spike. Simon tossed Andrew to the side and he collapsed on top of Amanda, clutching his arm. Simon had succeeded. The screaming had stopped.

Jeff took a few steps over to help Amanda with Andrew. Simon wiped the blood and sweat from his hands on to his pant legs and walked back over to join Kyle a few paces away.

The silence once again made the thumping sound in Kyle's head get louder. He closed his eyes and wished it away, but it was still there when he opened them. He looked around at the group and saw Amanda, Jeff, and Simon focusing their eyes directly behind him.

He turned around to face the largest pile of rubble. The marble was stacked nearly 8 feet high. It looked like the area that had been the hardest hit. Just beyond the pile, was the rest of the row of burial chambers, untouched. Kyle barely had time to wonder how they were still standing before the thumping noise got louder and louder.

Thump. Thump. Thump.

It wasn't in his head.

Thump. Thump. Thump.

He looked up at the florescent lights. It sounded to close to be coming from them. The sound seemed to change.

Pound. Pound. Pound.

Then Kyle realized why the entire crew was staring at the pile of marble ruin. His brother was still in the coffin trapped beneath

the marble.
		Pound. Pound. Pound.

10

Lyle was just as surprised as the rest of the crew
when the collapse happened. At first he figured
it was just Kyle and Simon playing another
prank on him by shaking the casket and
throwing pieces of marble at it. But the casket
began to shake harder and there was a loud
crashing sound outside.

He braced himself inside as the casket
rocked back and forth violently. Suddenly,
instead of a light swinging door, the lid to the
casket became heavy and it felt as though

someone had poured concrete on it.

Lyle braced his elbows against the back of the casket and pushed as hard as he could against the lid. It wouldn't budge. Something heavy was blocking it from the outside.

A wave of terror splashed over him as he realized he was trapped inside the casket. He closed his eyes and took a deep breath. He was sure this was just a way for Kyle to get him back. Kyle had recruited Simon to help him and they placed a few marble slabs over the coffin so Lyle couldn't get out.

But, that didn't explain the violent rocking. There was no way a human could knock this casket around that much.

Lyle began to pound on the front of the casket.

"Okay," he yelled. "You've had your joke. You got me back. Now, open this thing."

There was no response.

He pounded harder.

Still no response.

His breathing became faster and more erratic as he pounded harder on the casket. He quickly realized that this wasn't a joke his brother was pulling on him, this was real. Something outside was wrong and no one was responding to him.

The moment he realized it, the four walls of the casket began to close in around him. It was barely long enough for him to lay flat in, and the lid was merely inches from his face.

The plush ivory colored lining, which felt so comfortable only a few moments earlier, began to itch and push its way into his face.

He batted it away and noticed for the first time that he was sweating. That was a stark contrast to just 15 minutes ago when he was standing on his truck bed with his brother freezing as they gathered their tools.

The tools, Lyle remembered.

He was still wearing his tool belt. He maneuvered his hand down and grabbed the flashlight from his tool belt. He flicked it on and light flooded the inside of the casket.

Lyle thought that the light would make him feel better, but all it did was give him a better look at his surroundings. He began to panic even more when his eyes began to process the tiny space he was trapped in.

He pounded again on the top of the casket and yelled for help. No one responded.

Lyle's thinking became less rational the longer he was trapped. He was only in there for a minute or two but it began to feel like hours. The ideas began to run through his head. If there was no one to help him out, he was going to have to get himself out of here.

The lid was tightly sealed, so he needed to figure another way out. He reached down to feel around his tool belt. He felt a few screwdrivers and a hammer. An idea flashed in

Lyle's mind and he grabbed the hammer.

He wasn't able to get much swing since he was in such close quarters, but he had to try. He positioned his arm directly above him and drew it back as much as the casket would allow.

Lyle swung the hammer and struck the side of the casket with all of his might. The entire small box vibrated and Lyle cringed. He heard movement outside of the box. It sounded like debris shifting. He wondered again, what was going on out there?

He drew his arm back again and struck the side of the casket. He couldn't risk the top collapsing if there was something heavy on top of him.

Lyle was going to dig his way out from the side.

***

Before any of the crew could do anything, Kyle was down on his knees digging through the rubble. At first, everyone was too shocked to do anything. They just watched as Kyle tore through jagged pieces of marble and rotten wood.

Amanda came to her senses first. She was determined not to let her head injury get the best of her. She dropped to her knees next to Kyle and began to throw as much debris behind her as she could.

Jeff and Simon came next. They weren't quite sure where the casket was buried, but it didn't stop them all from digging through the ruins, desperately searching for Lyle.

Soon, all of the small pieces of marble had been removed and all that remained were several large pieces that had lined the walls of the burial chambers.

Kyle attempted to grab one, but he was unable to move it. Simon grabbed the other side of it, but it was still too heavy for them to move. Kyle kicked it and let out a guttural scream.

The mausoleum fell silent and the crew heard the pounding again. This time it was different. Louder.

Kyle began to walk around the giant pile of wreckage to try to get closer to the sound. He looked into every crevasse to figure out a way in. Through a very small hole near the bottom of the ruins, Kyle noticed a piece of marble vibrating. It shook with each pound. Kyle watched the marble to see what would happen.

The marble shook. Amanda, Jeff, and Simon filled in the small space behind him, trying to get a view of the shaking marble. With the next pound, the marble did more than vibrate. This time, the pounding cause the marble to fall over, revealing behind it a glimpse of the coffin.

***

The wood on the casket had begun to splinter. Lyle realized that it was going to get much more dangerous as the hammer began to penetrate the wooden side of the casket. He needed some way to protect his hand from the soon to be jagged wood.

Lyle placed the hammer on his chest and took several deep breaths. Each time he stopped to focus, the casket seemed to be getting smaller and smaller. Lyle laid his left arm at his side and used his right arm to begin pulling at his flannel shirt. He freed his left arm of the sleeve and did the same for his right. He pulled the shirt out from underneath him, careful not to tear it. He wrapped it around his right hand and returned to pounding his way out.

With the very next pound, the hammer smashed through the side of the casket. Lyle pulled it back inside to reveal a small hole, no more than an inch in diameter. A small amount of light flooded inside the space, and Lyle felt cool air rush inside.

He took a deep breath and it filled his lungs. Oxygen had never tasted sweeter. It reminded Lyle of biting into a cold slice of watermelon on a hot summer day.

Lyle squinted and looked through the hole. At first, the light hurt his eyes, but it quickly adjusted and through a mass of marble and black, moldy wood, he could see his brother staring back at him.

***

"Get me out of here," was the first thing Lyle heard after the hammer smashed through the side of the casket. It was so good to hear his brother's voice. He was alive. Kyle knew where he was. He would be able to save him.

Kyle laid down on the ground and lined his head directly up with the tunnel that led to the casket. The piece of marble that Lyle had knocked down only revealed a small piece of the coffin. Only a foot or so of it was revealed, and it was still several feet out of reach, thanks to all of the debris on top of it. It reminded Kyle of looking through a mouse hole on one of those old cartoons they used to watch as kids.

"We are going to get you out of there," Kyle yelled to his brother. "Are you hurt?"

"No," Lyle yelled back. "I'm okay, but this is freaking me out. You gotta hurry."

Kyle jumped back up so quickly, that the blood rushed to his head and made it difficult to see. He pushed through it and asked Jeff, "How can we get him out of here?"

Jeff looked past Kyle at the pile of rubble on top of the casket. They had removed all of the smaller pieces of marble. All that remained were several large pieces and a large wooden beam that must have been used to support the burial chambers.

The wooden beam was on top, with several large chunks of marble underneath it. Jeff figured the best way to removed this was to start at the top and work their way down. They couldn't risk the entire pile collapsing on top of the casket.

"We need to start with that beam," Jeff said, pointing to the top of the ruins.

"Are you out of your mind old man?" Simon chimed in. "There's no way the 5 of us can move that beam. Andrew can't even stand up."

The group had forgotten about Andrew. He was still lying on the ground clutching his shoulder. He appeared to be pretty out of it.

They turned their attention back to the task at hand.

"Maybe we could slide it off," Amanda suggested.

"If we do that, we run the risk of collapsing the entire thing," Jeff responded. "We don't know how stable this mound is."

"Well, we can't just leave him in there. We have to do something," Kyle pleaded. His voice was beginning to sound desperate.

Before the crew could come to a consensus, the pounding began again. Kyle fell back to the ground to find Lyle pounding on the side of the casket with the hammer again.

"Stop," Kyle yelled, but his voice was

obscured by the hammer.

Lyle was desperate to get out of the coffin. His mind wasn't working correctly. The only thing he could think about was getting out and standing up. A wave of panic set in over him and the only thing he could do to stop it was to start pounding again. He needed to get out, at any cost.

He drew his arm back as far as he could and struck the side of the casket. A piece of wood broke free and doubled the size of the hole. He struck it again and the hole got larger. Again. Again. The hole kept getting bigger. His plan was working.

His brother's voice echoed inside his head. "Stop," he heard Kyle saying, but the word had no meaning. Nothing had any meaning except getting out of the casket as soon as possible.

Lyle kept pounding until the hole in the side was nearly a foot long and 6 inches high. He could almost fit his face out, but resisted since the splinters jutted around the hole like razor wire.

Kyle screamed again, "Stop it Lyle," and the pounding stopped. With a small amount of fresh air and light, Lyle's brain began to work again. He understood his brother.

Kyle was on the ground no more than 2 feet in front of him, but he still was unable to get out. He could fit through the hole he had created. He couldn't fit through the mouse-hole tunnel. But, he could see Kyle. It was something.

"Lyle," his brother yelled to him, "we are going to get you out, but I need you to stop pounding and stay calm."

The eye contact with Kyle was all he needed to bring him focus. He relaxed as much as possible and dropped the hammer to his side.

Kyle motioned for Amanda to drop down to the ground next to him. "Stay with him for a minute," he said. Amanda nodded and looked a Lyle. Kyle stood up and turned to Jeff.

"We need to get him out of there fast. He's freaking out."

Jeff looked stumped. He wanted to think. Kyle turned to Simon.

"Let's just try Amanda's idea," Simon said. "The only way we're going to get him out of here is to move all of this shit, and that ain't happening until we get that beam off of the top."

Jeff butted in, "there's no way you can lift that beam."

"We're not going to lift it, we're just going to push it out of the way," Simon reasoned, turning back to Kyle.

Kyle bit his bottom lip. He had to get his brother out of there. They had no choice but to try.

"Let's do it," he said to Simon.

"This is not going to work," Jeff

screamed, but it was no use.

Simon jumped on the mountain of rubble and Kyle followed. The wooden beam was at the top, nearly eight feet off of the ground. They were careful not to slip on the shiny smooth marble. The mountain began to shake with every step and Lyle could feel every movement through his tiny surroundings.

With a panic in his voice he yelled to Amanda, "What is going on?"

She calming said back to him, "It's nothing to worry about. They are going to move the debris from off of you and we're going to get you out."

By the time she looked back up, Kyle and Simon had reached the top and positioned themselves on one side of the wooden beam. Amanda breathed a sigh of relief. It was so easy for them to get to the top, surely they would be able to move the wood beam easily and get Lyle out of there.

"Ready?" Simon said to Kyle. Their plan was to push the beam and roll it down the side of the debris.

Amanda reassured Lyle, "give them just a minute. They're digging you out."

Jeff stepped out of the way and positioned himself behind Amanda.

Simon counted down. "1. 2." He paused and looked at Kyle. "3!"

Both men pushed the wooden beam as

hard as they could. The marble beneath it cried out in pain as the beam began to move. It wasn't round, so it didn't move smoothly, but it moved. Kyle pushed harder and his end gained momentum slightly faster than Simon's. The beam crushed the marble beneath it as it made its first roll down the side of the debris.

Amanda looked up. It was working. It was her idea and it was working. The beam completed another rotation and was now nearly two feet from where it had started.

Kyle stood up as his grip on the beam loosened. It was on its way down now as gravity was doing all the work. He smiled. He was going to save his brother. When they were done and out of here they would go out for a beer and laugh about the whole thing.

Before Kyle was even able to finish his thought, something went wrong. The beam was no longer smoothly rolling down the side of the debris, it was now jerking wildly. It wasn't crushing marble any more; it was getting caught on it. Kyle wished it would just be over. Only 3 more feet and the beam would be on the ground.

The beam was heading directly for the large piece of marble that Simon and Kyle were trying to move earlier. The beam hit the top of the marble and drove it directly down into the rubble. There was a loud splintering sound and the entire mausoleum filled with Lyle's agonizing scream.

11

The sounds from outside the casket were terrible. Lyle cringed with every roll of the beam. The sound was getting closer and closer and before he could even move, something came crashing through the top of the casket, just above his legs.

Lyle felt a rush of pain and the casket rocked back and forth. Luckily, the lid held firm near his face and didn't crush him all together. He screamed as the pain rushed through his body and invaded his head. His breathing began to increase as he frantically searched again for the flashlight.

He found it lying next to him and brought it to life. He looked down at his legs. He couldn't see them. Whatever had crashed through the top of the coffin had crushed his legs just above the knee. Blood seeped from the impact area, and Lyle screamed again.

The pain was running through out his entire body. It came down over him hard like his hammer on the side of the casket. It was excruciating. He wondered if his legs had been severed or merely crushed. He tried to think of a way out, but his mind would not cooperate. He could focus on nothing but the pain.

Through the cloud of pain, he heard Amanda's voice. He couldn't make out what she was saying, but he turned to face her though the hole. When he turned his face, sweat dripped into his eyes. He hadn't noticed he had been sweating, but it must have been bad if it immediately hit him in the face.

"Lyle! Lyle!" It was his name she was yelling.

Soon, a deeper voice joined her, also yelling his name, "Lyle!" It was his brother.

He saw Amanda slide out of the way and made eye contact with his brother. It provided him with a small sense of comfort. That familiar face that he had known his entire life was there with him.

"Are you okay?" Kyle asked him.

Lyle tried to speak, but the words were difficult to form.

"Legs," he said. "My--" His mouth had gone too dry to speak.

The sweat dripped again into his eyes. Only this time he couldn't feel it. The pain that was blinding him began to dissipate. A wave of frigid nausea engulfed him and suddenly, despite his heavy sweating, he grew cold.

"We're going to get you out of there," Kyle barked, losing hope. "We're going to find some way to get you out of there."

After the cold took over, Lyle found himself able to speak. "This can't be happening to me," he said to Kyle.

"It's okay man. It's going to be okay."

"It was just a joke. We've always been playing jokes on each other. Ever since we were little. It never turned out like this. This isn't really happening, right Kyle?"

Kyle reached his hand far into the hole, trying to reach his brother.

Lyle reached out, with his shirt still wrapped around his hand, and grabbed his brother's hand.

"This can't be happening," he repeated. "It's gotten so cold in here. I'm so cold, Kyle."

Kyle grabbed the flannel shirt from his brother's hand and drew it out of the hole. He pushed himself up to his knees and pulled off his bright orange jacket. He flopped back to the ground and pushed it into the hole. He met Lyle's hand and gripped it around the jacket.

Lyle pulled the jacket through the hole in the casket and rested his head on it. He didn't have the strength to try to put it on. It smelled like Kyle. The smell took him back to his parent's house.

"This can't be happening."

He remembered the night that he and Kyle snuck out of the house for the first time.

He remembered the fights they used to get into as teenagers.

He remembered the party they threw after their high school graduation.

"This can't be happening."

It was getting harder to breath. The breath would no longer come naturally. Lyle had to concentrate on taking oxygen into his lungs.

He reached his hand back out of the hole and gripped his brother's hand. Kyle noticed how cold his brother's hand had become.

"This can't be happening," Lyle repeated one final time.

Lyle took a deep breath and used all of his strength to squeeze his brother's hand. Kyle squeezed back. He felt Lyle's grip loosen and his hand go limp.

"Lyle," Kyle screamed at him.

There was no response.

Lyle was glad that his brother had passed him his jacket. It brought back some wonderful memories for him. Lyle had spent his entire adult life trying to distance his identity from his brother's. But, the only thing that brought him comfort in the end, were the memories of their time together.

12

Kyle still had Lyle's shirt in his hand as he jumped up. He turned around and faced the crew. His face boiled with anger. The crew understood what happened. Kyle didn't need to say it. They all felt the same way as he did. They lost one of their own. They had been together so long they were like a big dysfunctional family. Kyle expressed his rage at the situation by kicking the wooden beam.

He lashed out, "this is all your fault Amanda. You were the one with the stupid idea to push that beam off."

Before the words even left Kyle's mouth, Amanda was feeling guilty. She was only trying to help. She should have listened to Jeff. If Jeff said it wasn't going to work, she should have agreed with him.

Instead, she was the one who put the idea in Kyle's mind. She knew he wasn't thinking rationally. He was focused only on saving his brother.

He pushed his way over to her and pressed his nose against hers.

"Lyle would still be alive now if it wasn't for you," he screamed, spraying her with saliva.

Simon pushed his way in between them. "It wasn't her fault that the building collapsed."

Amanda was stunned. Kyle must not be thinking rationally if Simon was the voice of reason. Kyle backed off, but his rage did not subside.

Jeff butted in. "What we need to focus on now is finding a way out of here. Turning on each other is not going to help. I think we've all seen what fighting leads to."

He was right. The group worked best together when they let Jeff lead them and kept the arguing to a minimum.

Kyle turned his back to the group. He distanced himself as far as he could. He looked down and saw Andrew on the ground. He had completely forgotten about him. Andrew's eyes were open now, and he appeared alert.

"The front door is completely blocked. There is no way we're getting out of there," Amanda said. "Is there another way out?"

Jeff looked down for his clipboard. It must have gotten lost in the collapse. "I don't know," he said. "I lost the blue print and Sandy's the only other one who has a copy."

Andrew sat up. He clutched his should with his uninjured hand. The bleeding seemed to have stopped.

"Call her then," Andrew reasoned. His voice was shaky.

Jeff reached down and grabbed his phone from his belt. Luckily, it was undamaged. He pressed and held number two, which was Sandy's speed dial, and pressed the phone to his ear.

Ring.

Kyle kicked again at the rubble. He held Lyle's shirt tight in his hand.

Ring.

Andrew balanced himself with his good hand, and made his way to his feet.

Ring.

Simon brushed sweat from his brow and wiped it on his pants. Even though the temperature in the mausoleum was frigid, he was still sweating like a pig in heat.

Ring.

Amanda caught Kyle looking at her. She

looked away quickly.

Ring.

Jeff took a deep breath. The mausoleum was silent. With the exception of Kyle, the entire crew was looking at him. They were counting on him to get them out of this mess.

"Hi. You've reached Sandy--" The phone was turned up loud enough that the entire crew could hear. Jeff hung up on the voicemail and placed it back in the holder around his belt.

"Shouldn't we call the police or something?" Amanda suggested.

Jeff thought for a moment before responding. "Even if we do, they aren't going to be able to get to us if there is no way in."

"They could dig us out," Amanda responded.

"It's too risky. Any more trauma to the building's structure could cause another collapse and put us in more danger."

"Sandy has the blue print, though."

"Then we need to get a hold of Sandy. I'll keep trying. But, in the mean time, I think we should see if we can find another way out."

It sounded like a good idea.

"I'll go," Simon offered.

"No," Jeff said. "No one should go off alone. We need to stick together."

"Fuck that," Simon said. "I don't need anybody's help to find my way out of this shit hole."

"He's right," Amanda said. By this point, she was willing to go along with just about anything Jeff said.

"I think--" Andrew said, but before he could finish his thought, he knees gave out and he fell back to the ground.

Amanda and Jeff ran over to him. His eyes were alternating between open and closed. He was sweating profusely and his shirt was soaked with perspiration.

"I think he's in shock," Jeff said.

"He's in no shape to moving around looking for a way out," Amanda objected.

"You're right," Jeff said. "Someone should stay with him, and the other three of us can go searching for a way out."

"I thought you just said we're not splitting up," Simon mumbled.

"Someone needs to stay here with Andrew," Jeff said firmly.

"I'm not doing it," Simon barked. "I'm gonna find a way out of here if it's the last thing I do."

"Amanda? Kyle?"

Kyle was still raging in the corner.

"I'll do it," Amanda volunteered.

"No," Kyle said softly. "I'm not ready to leave Lyle yet. I'll stay."

No one wanted to argue with him. Simon walked over to Kyle. At first, Amanda thought he was going to comfort him, but in one quick motion, Simon jerked the hatchet from Kyle's tool belt. Kyle didn't seem to notice.

Simon was the first one out. Since the rubble had cornered them in the front of the mausoleum, the only way out was over the rubble. Jeff followed him.

Amanda took a look back over her shoulder before she left. Kyle was still standing there. He had put on Lyle's shirt and was staring at the hole in the ruins. Andrew was still lying on the ground, head moving slightly.

She carefully climbed up the rubble, careful to avoid the splinters and shards of marble. She jumped off the other side and was soon walking down the hallway with Jeff and Simon towards the office area.

Kyle sat down on a slab of marble and put his hands in his head. He was so angry. How could he let this happen to his brother?

Kyle realized he should have listened to Jeff in the first place. This just angered him more. Why did he have to listen to Amanda's stupid idea? If he had told her to fuck off his brother would still be alive right now.

Kyle grabbed a small piece of marble from the ground, stood up, and threw it against the exterior wall of the mausoleum. It shattered into pieces and fell to the floor. Kyle let out his anger with a single guttural scream.

The sound brought Andrew back to consciousness.

13

Sandy walked down the long corridor. Door after door and they all looked the same to her. She hated the smell. It reminded her of death, and after the flower incident she had enough death for one day.

She was able to get an acceptable bouquet and she held it in her arm like a baby. The greenery wasn't as green as she would have liked. The colors not as vibrant, but it was the best she could do.

She couldn't remember which room it was she was looking for. She peered inside each one and just saw bed after bed of sick patients.

Hospitals gave her the creeps.

Sandy pulled her phone out of her purse. She knew she had a text message with the room number in it somewhere. She stopped in the hallway and leaned against a cool plastic railing. She searched through her phone and found the text. Her friend was in room 314.

She looked up just in time to see a nurse passing her by.

"I'm sorry ma'am," the nurse said. "All cell phones need to be turned off. They can interfere with the medical equipment."

"Oh, I'm sorry," Sandy responded back to her. She pushed the power button on her phone and pushed it down into her purse.

The nurse continued down the hallway as Sandy found that room 314 was just across the hallway. She walked over to the door, gave it a half hearted knock, and entered.

The room was dark and very warm compared to the cool air in the hallway. There was a small table lamp that was illuminating the room. As her eyes adjusted to the light, her friend Claire was laying in the small hospital bed. She had a variety of machines hooked up to her. Sandy recognized the I.V. and the heart monitors, but everything else looked very futuristic to her.

Sandy sat her flowers down on Claire's tray table, and sat down in the lone sterile chair next to her bed. Sandy wasn't sure if she was unconscious or simply sleeping. Either way, Sandy didn't want to bother her.

She sat in silence for a few minutes before the no-cell-phone nurse entered the room.

"Is she unconscious?" Sandy asked the nurse.

"She's sedated," the nurse responded. "Are you family?"

"Yes," Sandy lied. "She's my sister."

"She was very upset earlier after her talk with the doctor. We gave her something to help her rest," the nurse sympathized.

"What did the doctor say?"

The nurse hesitated, "I'm sorry. I can't discuss a patient's diagnosis with anyone. She'll have to tell you herself."

"Please," Sandy bargained. "She's my oldest and dearest friend. If something is wrong with her, she would want me to know."

The nurse made a deliberate gesture with her eyes to the end of Claire's bed. She pulled the curtain next to the bed to give Sandy some privacy and left the room.

Sandy stood up and walked to the end of Claire's bed. Her chart was hanging on the bottom of the bed. Sandy looked around but could see nothing except the curtain and Claire lying silently in the bed. There wasn't even a window in the room offering a ray of hope.

She picked up the chart and flipped it open. Claire's diagnosis was written at the top of the page.

Ventricular Septal Defect.

The words were foreign to Sandy. It must be pretty serious if it required that many big words. She looked back to Claire. She was asleep, and by the sounds of it was going to remain that way for quite some time. Sandy moved her flowers to Claire's bedside table, drew the curtain back, and walked into the hallway. She would come back later when her best friend was awake.

Sandy nearly bumped into the nurse, who was waiting just outside the door.

"Oh, excuse me," Sandy said, stepping around her. She took a step past the nurse and quickly twirled back to face her. "If a patient were to, hypothetically, have something called Ventricular Septal Defect. What would that mean?"

The nurse responded gently, "it would mean the patient has a hole in their heart."

14

Andrew drifted in and out of consciousness. He could remember bits and pieces of what happened. He remembered a loud crashing noise. He remembered Simon's demented face in front of him. He remembered unbearable pain in his shoulder. He remembered standing up, but he didn't remember how he got back on the ground.

His eyes once again came into focus and he saw a row of burial chambers above him. He didn't remember seeing these before. He forced himself to sit up. He saw the long hallway of burial chambers in front of him. He turned his head and caught a glimpse of the pile of rubble behind him.

He couldn't remember how he got here. Had he climbed the pile and ended up on the other side? Did the crew drag him over here? Where was the crew? He was alone in the hallway.

He felt sweat dripping off of his brow. He reached his hand up and used the sleeve of his shirt to wipe it off. As he lowered his arm, a flash of red blinded his vision. He looked around but couldn't see anything. He raised his hand again to wipe his forehead off. As he lowered his arm again, the same flash of red appeared.

Andrew's mind couldn't comprehend what he was seeing. He looked down at his hands and saw it. They were covered in blood. Was it his blood? Was his shoulder bleeding that much?

He reached up and gently touched the wound on his shoulder. It stung, but when he withdrew his hand no new blood appeared.

If this was his blood, surely it would have dried by now. The blood on his hands appeared fresh. It couldn't be his.

Andrew propped himself up against the row of burial chambers. He carefully used his good arm to push himself up off the ground. He stood, wobbly, and put one foot in front of the next. He was slowly making his way back to the office.

***

Simon tried the door again. It was still locked: that's why he brought Kyle's hatchet.

Amanda and Jeff were investigating the cedar plank wall. It looked sturdy, but out of place.

Simon swung the hatchet at the door. The first swing nicked the door, causing a small chunk of plywood to fly across the room. The noise caught Amanda and Jeff by surprise. Neither was against Simon's actions, they were all working towards the same goal, but it caught them off guard.

He swung the hatchet again and another chip from the door went flying. Amanda watched. Simon was swinging too high. The chips he was taking were from the top third of the door.

She chimed in, "swing lower, down near the handle."

Simon turned to glare at her.

"Just separate the knob from the door and it will swing right open," she stated flatly.

Simon knew she was right. He swung the hatchet again, this time aiming lower near the knob.

Amanda and Jeff turned their attention back to the cedar wall. Amanda attempted to grip one of the planks. They were tightly nailed in so she wasn't able to get a good grip on it. She tried putting her fingers in one of the knot holes, but the plank was attached firmly.

Jeff attempted to use his hands to pry off the end board, but also got no where.

He looked at Amanda, "when Simon gets that door open, we can use the hatchet to pry one of these boards off. There may be a way out behind these boards."

Simon chopped at the door again like a piece of flimsy firewood. He created a good size hole next to the door knob and was beginning to create a semi circle around it. He chopped the door a few more times before throwing the hatchet to the ground.

He grabbed the door knob and gave it a firm tug and it easily pulled off of the door, taking the chopped wood around it with it. Simon discarded the door knob and swung the door open.

Amanda and Jeff quickly crowded around him to see what was beyond the door.

It was a staircase. It led down into the darkness.

"Are you going down there," Amanda asked with a hesitation in her voice.

"No," Jeff responded. "We are."

"No, you're not," Simon fumed. "You two stay here and see what is behind that wall. I'll go down and see if there's a way out."

"I said we are going to stay together," Jeff demanded.

"I'm going," Simon said, and before Jeff had a chance to argue, Simon disappeared down the dark staircase.

"Let him go," Amanda said. She bent over and picked up the hatchet and returned to the cedar wall.

Jeff stood glaring down the staircase.

"Hey," Amanda yelled waking him from his trance. "Give me a hand over here."

Jeff hopped over to where Amanda was standing and helped her wedge the hatchet between the first plank in the cedar wall and the marble edge of the mausoleum. They both gripped it firmly and positioned themselves to get some leverage. Amanda met Jeff's eyes and gave him a nod. They both pulled with all of their might and the cedar plank began to crack. Splinters of wood popped off of the board and flew in every direction. Amanda closed her eyes as one whizzed past her head. It was beginning to work. They could feel the nails loosening and the plank began to twist.

"Keep going," Amanda dictated. "It's starting to loosen."

She was pulling with all of her might. The hatchet got harder and harder to pull. At first Amanda thought the board was resisting, but she soon realized that Jeff had stopped pulling.

"What are you doing?" She asked, looking up at him. She noticed his gaze was fixed on the doorway of the office. Amanda loosened her grip on the hatchet and looked over her shoulder.

Andrew was standing in the doorway of the office, blood dripping from his hands.

15

"What happened to you," Amanda asked, pulling the hatchet out of wall.

"I don't know," Andrew responded. "I just woke up this way."

"Are you hurt?" Jeff worried.

They ran over to the doorway and began to survey Andrew for any further damage. The bleeding from his shoulder had stopped and began to dry on his shirt. His left arm hung loosely at his side. He wasn't able to move it without causing himself a great deal of pain.

"Other than your shoulder, you appear to be okay," Jeff deduced.

"Where is Kyle?" Amanda asked.

"I don't know. I don't know what happened. I just woke up and walked back here."

Jeff's eyes met Amanda's. They both had a strange notion to check on Kyle.

"Here," Amanda said. "Come over here and sit down."

She tucked the hatchet under her arm, grabbed Andrew on his good shoulder, and led him to the creaky chair behind the desk. "We're going to go check on Kyle. Stay put. You're in no condition to be moving. We'll be back in a minute."

Andrew nodded. It was biggest reaction he could muster up the strength for.

Amanda handed the hatchet to Jeff and they left the relative cozy comfort of the office and headed back into the icy cold mausoleum.

Jeff walked with a purpose and Amanda struggled to keep pace. She was seeing clearer now than she had immediately after the collapse, but she still felt like she was functioning at half capacity.

"Should we try to call Sandy again?" Amanda suggested.

"Good idea," Jeff responded and pulled his cell phone from the holder on his belt. He held down number two and placed it to his ear. It rang. It rang again. It rang again. Amanda could hear each ring as the sound pierced through her aching skull. Jeff's phone was loud enough to hear from the other side of the mausoleum.

Jeff got Sandy's voicemail again.

"No answer," Jeff said.

"How long do we wait before we just call 911 for them to come get us out of here?" Amanda asked.

"It still won't do much good without the blue prints. But, if we don't find a way out behind that wall or in the basement, we'll call."

They had reached the pile of ruins that separated them from where Kyle was waiting.

Jeff began the climb first. He was amazed at the ease at which they were able to get over the pile. It was almost as if it had fallen in such a way to give them easy access in and out.

He reached the top and turned around to give Amanda a hand. She was slowly making her way up. Jeff reached out his hand and gave her the pull she needed to make it to the summit.

They stood at the top looking down into the semi circle that trapped them not long ago. Jeff noticed first the pool of blood from where Andrew had been laying. Amanda immediately saw Kyle. He was lying in his side looking directly into the rabbit hole where his brother died. He was wearing Lyle's shirt.

Jeff started down the other side and Amanda quickly followed. They stopped when they got to Kyle's feet.

"Kyle," Jeff said. He did not respond.

Amanda wondered what it would be like to lose a brother. She was an only child, so she could only imagine the horror Kyle must be feeling right now.

"Kyle," Jeff repeated, slightly louder this time.

"Maybe we should just leave him alone, Jeff. He's going through a hard time."

"Kyle," Jeff tried his name one more time.

"Come on Jeff, he obviously just wants to be alone."

Jeff gave Kyle's leg a small kick and it fell over to the side causing his body to twist at an unnatural angle.

Amanda realized it as soon as Jeff said it, "something's wrong."

Jeff leaned down and grabbed Kyle by the shoulder. He pulled firmly and forced Kyle over onto his back.

Amanda first saw a long thing piece of red wood move in synch with Kyle. Her brain wasn't moving fast enough to process what it was until Kyle was flat on his back.

Kyle was dead. There was an ax sticking straight out of his forehead. Amanda's brain finally caught up with her eyes and she screamed. Jeff grabbed her and squeezed. It provided her little comfort.

She could see inside of Kyle's skull. The ax had splintered his head. It looked to Amanda like a cracked open walnut. Inside, there was a mass of pulpy white matter. A steady stream of blood still flowed from the wound. It covered the left side of his face and began to drip onto the shiny pale marble floor.

"Who would do this?" Amanda screamed in desperation.

Jeff pulled her out of their embrace by her shoulders and looked directly at her. He knew if he gave her a minute, she would come to the same conclusion that he had.

She was too upset to think.

"Andrew," Jeff said.

"No," she cried, shaking her head back and forth. "He wouldn't do anything like this."

"There was blood all over his hands," Jeff said.

"No," she repeated. "There's no way."

Jeff suddenly realized that they had left Simon alone, exploring the basement.

"Simon," he called out. He pushed Amanda away from him and ran towards the pile of rubble.

Amanda had to confess. She knew something she wasn't telling Jeff.

"Jeff. Wait." Amanda yelled at him. He turned to face her. "Andrew isn't even supposed to be here."

16

Simon walked carefully down the warped wooden staircase. There was very little light to guide him down the stairs. He warily went down one stair at a time until the floor underneath him felt solid. He knew he had reached the bottom.

The little light that was coming from the top of the stairs had gone, and Simon was standing in total darkness. He reached into his pocked and pulled out his cell phone. He mashed the keypad with his thumb and the screen glowed to life. He held it out in front of him to see what was at the bottom of the stairs.

In the dim glow coming from his phone screen, Simon was able to see a hallway in front of him. He cautiously put his hand on the wall and began to walk down the narrow passageway.

The glow from the phone provided just enough light to see a few feet in front of him. He wasn't able to tell how long the hallway was or where it was leading him.

Simon took a few more steps and the cell phone suddenly went dark. The screen had gone to sleep. Simon pushed the key pad again and the screen roared back to life.

He kept his hand firmly on the wall, using it to guide him. His hand hit something hard on the wall, and he turned his phone to investigate. His hand hit a door frame.

Simon reached down and tried the handle. It was rusted and cold, but turned easily in his hand. He pushed open the door and stuck his hand inside to illuminate the room.

It was another small office. The room was so tiny that the phone had no trouble lighting up the room. The room contained no furniture except for a small desk. Simon was about to enter the room to investigate, but the screen again went black, leaving him in complete darkness.

He rethought his purpose. This was not time to investigate. He was trying to find a way out. This was obviously not it, so he decided to keep moving. He left the door to the room open, hit the keypad again, and started back down the hallway.

No more than two feet later, he hit another doorway. He grabbed the doorknob again and threw open the door: another office.

This one was stacked full of old furniture. Simon held the phone out in front of him as far as he could to get a better look into the room.

There were several desks stacked on top of each other. Next to the desks, there was a pile of chairs that was nearly 6 feet tall. They were a jumble of worn brown leather and rusty legs.

The phone went black again, and Simon brought it back to life.

He took a deep breath and continued along the hallway. He was beginning to get discouraged. The only thing he had found so far was a bunch of empty offices. He started to lose hope that he was going to find a way out.

Simon warily placed his hand back on the wall. He held the phone out in front of him like a shield and continued down the hallway. This time, he could see the end. It was a dead end. There was nothing more to be found down here.

He was about to turn around and head back to the stairs, when he noticed on the opposite side of the hallway there was a lone door. Simon cautiously stepped across the hallway and stood in front of the door. He reached down for the door knob. His calloused hand didn't notice, but the rust on this door knob was worse than the rest.

Simon gripped the knob with one hand, and held the phone out in front of him in the other. He slowly turned the knob and the clanking of the lock vibrated throughout the hallway. The door let out a sigh and slowly began to move from its resting position.

Just as he pushed open the door, the cell phone screen again went black. He felt the door open fully and he pushed the keypad again.

The screen sparked to life and Simon was startled to see he was standing face to face with another person. It startled him and he tumbled backwards and fell out into the hallway. He let out a brief yelp on the way down. He saw the figure in front of him raise something above his head and Simon was suddenly blinded with pain.

The last thought that ran though his mind before he lost consciousness was that he recognized the face in front of him.

17

"What do you mean Andrew isn't supposed to be here?" Jeff fumed.

"He called me last night. Somehow he had heard about the job and needed money, so he wanted in on it," Amanda responded.

"And?" Jeff was getting angrier.

"So," Amanda hesitated. "I told him about it."

Jeff's face turned a bright shade of red. "You brought him here?"

Amanda looked down, she was ashamed. "We've done it another time or two. We didn't think anyone would notice."

"I think Kyle noticed," Jeff seethed.

Amanda felt a wave of guilt ride up her spine and settle in the back of her throat. She couldn't face the fact that she had invited Andrew here and he killed Kyle. She pushed the thought so far in the back of her mind that it was hidden by the guilt she was feeling.

"I'm sorry Jeff. It's not like we couldn't use the extra help, right?"

Jeff thought about it for a second. "Wait, he said. You're wrong. Sandy called him. She told me we needed five men." He counted on his hand. Lyle. Kyle. Simon. Amanda. Andrew. "Yes," he said. "That's five."

"I think she was counting you in that five," Amanda said. "That's how we were able to get around it in the past. Sandy always counted you in the number, but I don't think you ever realized it."

Jeff was furious. He thought his crew was with him on all of these jobs, but he suddenly felt betrayed. He only had enough money to keep a few of them around, and now they were trying to take him for what little money he had left.

He wasn't usually an angry man. Especially about things like money that he couldn't control. Jeff always had his ups and downs over the years. There were a few years back near the beginning of Crane Construction that he didn't even have enough to make ends meets. But Sandy did wonders for his business. She was very social throughout high school and college. They came from a small town and Sandy knew everyone. They knew her and trusted her. As soon as she put her mind to it, he was getting calls left and right to make bids. And most of the time, he got them.

Jeff expanded the business rapidly and it began to grow. At one point, he had hundreds of people on his payroll. They were booking jobs as far away as Dayton or Scranton and his personal bank account grew into the seven-digit range. For a guy from small town New Castle, PA who went to Slippery Rock University and majored in partying, this was a big deal.

When the economy turned down earlier in the decade, things started to get worse. He saw the competition come in with lower bids. Everyone was desperate to book a job, and the customers were no longer willing to pay for the jobs. There was undercutting everywhere. Most of the crew moved on, and Jeff was stuck. It hurt him the most to let Sandy go. If it wasn't for her, he wouldn't have been able to keep Crane going for so long. This was their first Monday on a job without Sandy, and Jeff hadn't been able to get this thought out of his mind all day.

"Do you really think Andrew could have done this?" Amanda agonized.

"I don't know Amanda, they only two people in here with us are him and Simon."

"We've know him for years Jeff, there's no way he could."

"Simon," Jeff screamed.

In all the excitement, they forgot about Simon.

"We left him alone down those stairs," Jeff cried out. "We've got to get to him before anything can happen."

Jeff jumped up began to climb the mountain of rubble.

Amanda screamed at him, "Wait!"

Jeff stopped and turned to face her.

"If someone really did kill Kyle, don't you think we should have a weapon?"

Jeff took a deep breath. That was the Amanda he known all of these years. Smart and cool under pressure. Always thinking two steps ahead. Working with him, instead of against him.

"You're right," he barked, jumping off of the rubble. He looked around near his feet. "What can we use?"

Amanda looked over at Kyle's body, trying to get Jeff to notice it. He was too busy looking around in the debris. He bent over and picked up a piece of marble, but threw it back to the ground. He tried a piece of wood, but it crumbled in his fingers.

"Jeff," Amanda called to get his attention. He looked over at her, and she again glanced down at Kyle's body.

He still didn't get it. She was going to have to spell it out to him.

"We have an ax right here," she hesitated.

Jeff looked down at Kyle. He shook his head back and forth. "No," he bellowed. "We can't use that. We have to leave him alone."

"Do you have a better idea?" Amanda asked.

"Here," Jeff said, bending down over Kyle's body. He reached into Kyle's tool belt and pulled out a hammer. "We can take this."

"Look, if someone is in here with us, and they had this ax somewhere, don't think they have a variety of other options that are going to make this little hammer pretty useless?" She was forceful.

Jeff thought for a minute. "What about the hatchet? We left that in the office. We can use that too."

"We can grab that," she said. "But, we left Andrew in there, don't you think that if he wanted that he would have grabbed it by now?"

She had a point. Jeff was convinced the ax was a good idea, in theory, but he didn't want to disturb Kyle's body.

"You win," Jeff said. "Just do it quickly."

Amanda didn't hesitate. She turned to

Kyle and gripped the handle of the ax in her hands. She gave it a brief wiggle to judge exactly how much force was necessary. She gave Jeff a final look over her shoulder and placed her foot directly in the center of Kyle's chest. She took a deep breath in and quickly jerked the ax forward. It easily dislodged from Kyle's head.

Jeff tried not to look, but couldn't help catching a glimpse of a piece of Kyle's skull hitting the bitter marble floor.

18

Simon was in bed. It was cold outside and the heat never quite got to warm in the old farmhouse. He pulled the covers up above his head and embraced the warmth that surrounded him. He wished his body would fall back to sleep, but the bright light that was coming though his window forced its way through the blanket and shined in his eyes.

He put his forearm over his face to try to block it. He captured a few moments of peace before he heard yelling coming from outside his door.

"Simon," the voice yelled, harsh and raspy.

He closed his eyes tighter, wishing he could make it go away.

"Simon," it called again.

He threw the covers back and hopped out of bed so fast his head began to spin. The cold floor of the farmhouse stung his feet and he quickly hopped on the dirty rug that sat next to his bed. He rubbed his eyes and tried to catch his balance.

"I'm coming," he yelled blindly.

Simon walked over to the door and turned the knob. It moaned in pain and slowly allowed the chipped wooden door to open. Simon stepped out into the hallway and made his way to a flight of stairs. He carefully stepped down them one at a time, holding on to the solid oak railing.

It may have been the head rush from standing up, or maybe he was still just half asleep, but his brain wasn't allowing him to see clearly yet.

The stairs led him to the first floor and directly to the front door. He quickly made a right and headed into what used to function as a living room. It now looked more like a hospital room.

There was a hospital bed in the center of

the room. Attached to it were several monitors and an IV bag. In the bed, laid a frail looking woman attached to a mass of wires. She was only in her 50s but she appeared much older. Her grey hair was pushed back into a bun, but looked as though it had not been washed in weeks.

Her arms were as thin as a pretzel and were left badly bruised from the endless needles. Her eyes were sunken and dark. Simon often felt his eyes looked the same way. The woman wore an oxygen mask over her face and only removed it when she spoke.

A small television sat in front of the bed showing an undistinguishable morning show. The hosts rattled on about the latest fashion trends and movie stars.

"Simon," the old woman called again.

"Yes, mom," he responded. He took a few steps towards her hospital bed. The light again shined brightly through the front window. Simon again tried to block it with his forearm, but it pierced his vision and caused a murkiness in his brain.

"Simon," his mother bellowed. "It's 6AM. I've been up for hours. I need my breakfast."

Simon sighed. "Okay, mom. I'll get it for you."

Simon stumbled over to the kitchen. He pulled two slices of wheat bread from a bag on the counter and pushed them down into the toaster. He quickly heated up some hot water in a beat up microwave and used half for a cup of tea and half for a bowl of hot cereal.

He placed the food on a tray and returned to the living room. He placed the tray on a moving stand and wheeled it in front of his mother.

"Thank you," she said.

Simon stumbled back across the living room, light hitting him in the eyes again, and made his way back up the stairs.

He returned to his bedroom, pushed the door shut behind him, and returned to the relative comfort of his bed.

The bright light coming from the window again pierced his eyes. He tossed and turned but the light would not go away. His mind still hazy, he again tried to close his eyes. He wanted nothing more than to go back to sleep, but the light would not allow him.

He tried to move his forearm again to cover his face but it wouldn't move. He looked down and it was bound to his side. He tried his other arm. It was also bound. He couldn't move. He looked up and again the light blinded him.

Simon realized that he wasn't in his own bed. His mind suddenly became clearer. The light wasn't coming from outside his window. It was coming from a flashlight that someone was shining in his eyes.

He must have been dreaming of being home. And now that he realized where he was, this place was nothing like home.

Simon was strapped to an old wooden desk. His hands were bound to the sides of the desk. He tried to move his legs, but they too were tied to the desk.

The flashlight left his line of sight and his eyes began to adjust to the dark room.

"Let me out of here," was the first thing that escaped his mouth.

No one responded.

Simon slowly began to absorb his surroundings. He was in one of the small rooms under the mausoleum.

"If you don't let me out of here, I'll fuc--"

A voice cut him off. "You'll what"

"I'll kill you," he raged.

"You can't kill me. I'm going to kill you," the voice calmly emitted.

"Fuck you," he screamed.

"Simon," the voice said. "Is that any way to speak to me?"

He finally caught a glimpse of who was speaking. It was the same familiar face that flashed before he was hit on the head.

"Slate?" he asked.

"Yes," the voice said. "It's me."

19

"Try to call Sandy again," Amanda suggested as they walked along row of burial chambers on the way to the office. Amanda was carrying the ax and Jeff was holding the hammer in his hand.

Jeff reached down into his belt and pulled out his phone. He hit Sandy's speed dial and it began to ring.

Ring

"Jeff," Amanda stammered. "I-I'm sorry if I caused any of this."

Jeff's rage had subsided a little. He was thinking more clearly.

"It's not your fault Amanda. None of us could have known something like this was going to happen."

Ring

"I know that. That's what my head is screaming. But it's not what I'm feeling."

"Amanda," Jeff intercepted. "Don't let this worry you right now. We've got to concentrate on finding Simon and Andrew and getting a way out of here."

"Yes, I know."

Ring

"I don't know who did this, or why, but I do know that being trapped in here is beginning to get to all of us. We need to find a way out and let the police sort this out."

Ring

"If it was Andrew, do you think I'll be in trouble," Amanda shrieked.

"No. Just stay calm. Even if you were the one who asked him to come here, you didn't ask him to come here and kill someone. Did you?"

"Of course not!" Amanda quipped. "I had no idea what was happening. You and I found the body together."

Ring

"Nothing," Jeff said, hanging up the phone.

They rounded the corner at the end of the

burial chambers and noticed the door to the office had been closed.

"We didn't leave it like that," Amanda asked. "Did we?"

"No," Jeff responded. "We ran out here and left it open."

"Do you think Andrew is inside there?"

"I'm sure he is. We need to be very careful when we go in."

"I have an idea. You stand next to the door and throw it open, I'll stand there with the ax out in front of me in case he tries to jump out."

"Are you sure about that?" Jeff asked.

"Yes," Amanda answered. "I'm the reason he is here, I will be the one to take the risk."

Jeff quietly took a few steps over to the doorway. Once he got close to it, he could see that someone had just pushed the door shut, it wasn't latched. He pointed at the lock to Amanda and shook his head back and forth.

She was prepared. She had taken her place in front of the door and held the ax out in front of her. Some of Kyle's blood had dried on the handle and Amanda positioned her hand to avoid it. It didn't give her the best grip on the ax, but she couldn't bring her self to touch it.

Amanda gave Jeff a quick acknowledging nod. He looked her in the eye and counted down with a series of nods.

One.
Two.
Three.
Jeff threw open the door.

***

"I've always hated being called by my last name," Slate said.

"I'll call you whatever the hell you want me to, just get me off of this table," Simon squeaked.

"No," Slate said. "That would be too easy."

"What is your problem? Lyle is dead and I'm just trying to find a way out of this hell hole." Simon was losing his limited patience.

"There is no way out of this hell hole. If you would listen to what I'm saying, you would know that."

Simon watched as Slate walked over to the corner of the room and grabbed something. He couldn't see exactly what it was because Slate held it below his sight line.

"What is that?" Simon barked.

Slate walked over to him.

"Do you know the damage you've done to this crew over the years?" Slate asked him.

"What the hell are you talking about? I work my ass off for Jeff."

"You've also caused a lot of collateral

damage over the years. Your attitude sucks."

Simon opened up a little bit. "You don't know anything about my life. If you had to put up with half of the shit I do, you'd go fucking crazy."

"Oh," Slate responded. "You're talking about your frail mother."

"Shut the fuck up," Simon fumed. It was obvious it was a sore spot. "You don't know anything about my life or my mother."

"I know she did this to herself."

"You don't know shit."

"She smoked like a chimney for all of those years. Now her lungs have just given up on her. Tired of all of the years of abuse," Slate crooned. "Speaking of abuse, how did you put up with it all of those years?"

Simon raged. He thrashed and yanked, trying to free himself from his bonds. He screamed, but it was no use. No one could hear him through the thick layer of marble in the mausoleum.

"My mother was a great woman. It wasn't easy raising three boys on her own."

"Aw," Slate cooed, "Still defending her after all of the years."

"You don't know the first thing about it."

"I do know that the regular distractions you've caused over the years have left countless people damaged," Slate stated coldly.

Simon grew silent. His arms were still

pulling with all of his might, but Slate succeeded in getting his attention. The thin rope began to cut into his left wrist. The bright red marks on his skin slowly began to secrete blood.

"Do you remember that girl?" Slate asked.

"What girl?" Simon responded.

"Oh, wow. What was her name?" Slate asked knowingly, coyly. "Poor girl got her fingers broke. With one of these--"

Simon saw what Slate was holding below his sight line. It was a sledgehammer.

"What are you doing with that?" Simon asked, his voice beginning to quiver.

"The same thing you did to--"

Simon cut Slate off with the girl's name, "Elizabeth."

"Then this is for Elizabeth," Slate said calming.

Before Simon even had a chance to react, Slate raised the sledgehammer high in the air and brought it down on Simon's right hand.

Simon screamed as he heard the snapping noise, but the pain had not yet hit him. It was almost as if his body was blocking it out. He gathered up the courage to look down and he saw the damage to his body.

His hand was mangled. It hung unnaturally to the right. His wrist was snapped in half and a white shard of bone protruded through the skin. A small amount of blood had begun to pool on the desk, and before Simon could process it, the pool began to grow.

Just as he saw the damage, the pain registered in his brain and came over him like a wave. Between the agonizing pain and sight of blood, he felt light headed and nauseous. He tried to scream but bile backed up from his stomach and choked him in his throat. He turned his head to the left and tried to swallow it back.

Another scream escaped his lungs and forced some bile out of his mouth and onto the stale wooden desk.

"Now you're starting to know what it feels like," Slate said, returning the sledgehammer to its home in the corner of the room.

Simon tried to form words, but they would not come. His brain was overpowered with pain and could not process.

"Believe it or not, that was one of the simple injuries you've caused. There were a lot more." Slate paused. "Bloodier ones."

Simon looked up and met Slate's eyes. He shook his head back and forth. He noticed for the first time that Slate was holding a dull knife. The handle was made of faded wood and the metal of the blade was serrated with a hint of rust.

"Please," Simon was able to expel. "Please don't do this?"

"Do what? You don't even know which surprise injury we are going to replicate next."

"I don't deserve this," Simon quivered. "I didn't mean to cause any of those."

"Sure," Slate said. "I believe you. I know you didn't mean to cause any of them. But had you not been so distracted and arrogant every day, none of them would have happened."

"Please," Simon begged.

Slate continued, "Do you remember Kyle?"

Simon cringed. He knew exactly where Slate was going with this.

"Poor Kyle. He was so distraught and angry over his brother's death, he didn't even see me coming up behind him with that ax."

Simon closed his eyes to try to escape it, but all his mind could focus on was Kyle.

"But," Slate continued. "He saw you coming that day, didn't he? And you were ruthless. That scar on his ear. You never even flinched, did you?"

"Please, please don't do this," Simon quivered.

"Let's see if you flinch now." Slate took the rusty knife and began to slice at Simon's ear.

***

Amanda stared into the darkness. Someone had turned off the lights in the office.

She stood, perched outside the doorway, ax in hand, waiting to strike. Jeff stood next to the doorway staring at Amanda's face for any reaction. He didn't want to risk looking into the room and giving away his position.

She pushed the ax further out in front of her, and took two steps toward the doorway. She attempted to focus her eyes into the darkness but she could not make anything out in the small office.

Amanda felt like she did as a kid. The basement in her house always scared her. Her father would go down there for hours, but she was terrified of it. It always seemed so dark and smelled musty. This sensation was coming back to her now as she stood outside the office door. The stale air smell coming from inside over powered her. It took her back to five years old, standing outside her basement door.

She was never able to go down into that basement without her mom to hold her hand. Here she was, decades later, and she found her self in the same situation. She took a deep breath and the stale air filled her lungs. She resisted the urge to cough it out and took a step into the dark office.

A sense of accomplishment replaced the stale air in her lungs. She conquered the office. She carefully took one hand off of the ax and fumbled around on the wall next to her, looking for the light switch. Her hand found it and the single light bulb at the top of the office flicked to life.

Amanda took another deep breath, this time only stale air found her. The sense of accomplishment was gone and the terror was back.

The room was empty.

Andrew was missing.

She took a few steps to allow herself to see behind the desk.

Nothing.

"Jeff," she called out.

Jeff jumped into the doorway, ready for an attack. The hammer perched in his hand, high above his head.

He looked around the room and saw emptiness.

"Where did Andrew go?" Jeff asked.

"I don't know," Amanda responded. "But it looks like he took the hatchet."

***

Simon was glad he couldn't see what Slate had done to him. But, he could feel it. Suddenly, the pain of his hand didn't seem so bad. Slate had ruthlessly taken his ear. Sawed through it with a rusty blade and left it on the desk next to him. He had never done anything as ruthless to Kyle. It was a misunderstanding. Not exactly an accident, but a misunderstanding.

"I think you've suffered enough," Slate said, standing over him.

"Thank you, please, just let me go."

"No. That's not what I meant. I meant it's finally time to put you out of your misery for good."

"Please, just let me go." Simon reiterated. He was aware in his mind how flimsy and clichéd it sounded, but he couldn't think of anything else to say through the pain.

"I have one more thing I want to show you." Slate walked back to the corner of the room, reached down into the darkness of the floor, and pulled out a large shard of rotten wood from the burial chambers. "This is a really big splinter."

"No," Simon attempted to scream, but it came out as more of a whisper. Simon, once again, knew what was coming next.

"You can't think of a time when your negligence caused someone harm with a wooden splinter, can you?" Slate cooed.

"I will do anything. I need to get out of here." Simon was desperate.

"You need to get out of here?" Slate was getting angry. "So, what? You can return to your pathetic life."

"My mother needs me. Please, I will do anything you ask. Please, just let me know."

"You and this disgusting excuse for a group of humans ruined my life," Slate cried out angrily.

"Please, I will do anything," Simon bargained.

"You can tell me what you did. What did you do? What happened with a wooden splinter?"

"Not this," Simon tried again. "Anything but this…"

"What did you do?" Slate screamed at him.

"I--" Simon hesitated. A tear formed in his eye. "I caused him to get a wooden splinter in his…"

"In his what?"

"..in his eye." Simon finished.

"Who?" Slate screamed at him.

"Please, I will do anything, just let me--"

"WHO?"

Simon sobbed. "Andrew."

Slate laughed. "You've brought so much destruction to everyone's life. You expect me to just let you walk out of here so you can continue on your self destructive path? Well, guess what, asshole? Everybody's life sucks. Why do you get a pass? Does your life suck more than mine? You have no idea what I've lost."

Slate raised the wooden splinter high above Simon's head.

"Please, I'll do anything," Simon cried out.

"Anything?"

"Yes, anything." Simon bawled.

"How about just fucking die then?" Slate screamed and slammed the wooden shard down.

20

"We need to find Simon, and we need to find a way out of here," Amanda demanded.

"What about Andrew?" Jeff asked.

"Do you think we should be looking for him too?"

"Yes. He's part of the crew. He's one of us until it's proven otherwise."

Amanda wasn't sure she agreed, but she was willing to go along with Jeff.

"We need to get down in that basement

then," Amanda decided.

She pointed to the chopped up wooden door.

"I'll go first," she said to Jeff.

"No, I can't let you do that, I will go first."

"I have the ax," she said.

"But I have the only light," he said, pulling his cell phone from his pocket. "Stay right behind me, just in case."

Amanda reluctantly agreed.

Jeff took the lead and walked over to the staircase. Amanda followed closely behind. As Jeff began his descent down the stairs, Amanda held the ax firmly with one hand and the back of Jeff's shirt with the other.

Jeff held his cell phone out in front of him with one hand and gripped the hammer with the other. He carefully took one step at a time until he and Amanda reached the bottom.

As soon as they hit the solid concrete ground, Jeff noticed a doorway in front of him. He kept his finger firmly on a button to ensure his cell phone would not go dark. He motioned to Amanda, and they took their positions. Jeff stood next to the door with the hammer, and shined the phone at the door. Amanda stood in front of the door, ax in hand.

Jeff counted to three by nodding and threw open the door. The light from the cell phone flooded the room, and Amanda could quickly see that the room was empty. She nodded to Jeff to continue and he led the way down the hallway.

They quickly came to another door on the left and assumed the same strategy. As Jeff threw open the door, Amanda quickly noticed the room, while full of scrap furniture, was devoid of human life.

Jeff came to the end of the hallway and led Amanda to the other side. They quickly came upon another door and assumed their positions. Amanda gripped the ax in her hand. In the split second before Jeff threw open the door, Amanda got a different feeling about this one. A metallic smell filled the air and Amanda could not shake a feeling of dread. Jeff counted down with a series of nods.

One.

Two.

Three.

He threw open the door and the light from the phone filled the small room. Amanda saw the horror in front of her face and screamed. The strength in her arms fell away and the ax fell by her side.

Jeff jumped in front of her, hammer in hand, ready to strike and quickly saw Simon, lying dead on the table, face mangled, blood dripping from the desk onto the floor. He turned to Amanda and gripped her tight. She was still facing the horrific sight when Jeff grabbed her and turned her away.

It killed her to see Simon lying there like that, but she could not look away. Her eyes kept trying to go back to the room, even as Jeff was spinning her back to it. They clung to each other and tried to forgot what they saw, but the image of Simon, wooden shard sticking out of his eye, was forever engrained in their brains.

Jeff grabbed Amanda on either side of her head and forced her to focus on him. "We need to get out of here now."

Amanda agreed. She wanted nothing more than to get out of the basement.

Jeff grabbed her by the hand, cell phone leading the way, and pulled her towards the staircase. She was nearly there, when she realized she had let go of the ax.

"Jeff," she stopped him. "I left the ax lying back there."

"Stay right here," he responded. "I'll go back and get it."

Jeff let go of Amanda's hand and took a few steps back to where Amanda had dropped the ax. He used the phone to illuminate the ground. He noticed that bloody footsteps led from the room where Simon lay, back down the hallway, and up the stairs. Jeff leaned over and grabbed the ax in the same hand as the hammer, and walked back over to Amanda.

"These footsteps weren't here before, were they?" She asked him.

"I don't think so. Here, take the ax," he

said, handing it to her. "Stay right behind me."

Jeff made his way to the foot of the staircase and began up it. Near the top, he placed his cell phone back into the holder around his belt. The light from the office slightly illuminated the stairs and he didn't want to give it away to anyone that they were coming.

He cautiously stepped up into the office with Amanda directly behind him. They looked down at the ground at the same time and notice the bloody footprints were even more distinct on the pure white marble.

They led from the staircase, over to the small bathroom door, then around the desk and out into the main area of the mausoleum.

"Let's check the bathroom first," Amanda suggested.

Jeff led the way over to the bathroom. They assumed their attack positions. Jeff nodded to three and pushed on the door. He couldn't open it. It wasn't locked, but there was something blocking it. Jeff tried again and the door only opened an inch.

"Stay close behind me," Jeff mouthed to Amanda.

He placed the hammer in one of his belt loops and used both hands to push against the door. The door slid open about six more inches, but something was blocking it from opening any further.

"I'm going to look inside," Jeff mouthed

again, as Amanda looked on in horror.

Jeff propped the door open with his foot to make sure no one could close it. He grabbed the hammer again and propped it up in front of his face. He slid the hammer in through the crack in the door and slowly followed with his head.

He couldn't see anything except the sink and the toilet. Whatever was blocking the door from opening was still behind it. He stretched his head in far enough so that he could peer behind the door.

Jeff saw what was behind the door just in time for it to go slamming shut against his head.

21

Sandy was back in the small hospital room. Once she realized just how serious Claire's condition was, she knew it was important to be there for her friend when she woke up. Sandy was worried for her friend. They went back all the way to kindergarten.

Claire was the most popular girl in school, which wasn't hard to do in kindergarten. She had the best toys, always had the answers to the questions the teachers asked, and her parents sealed her fate with a pony at her sixth birthday party.

From day one, she took Sandy under her wing. Sandy was very shy back in those days and would not have the courage to speak to anyone. Claire would always do the speaking.

They remained close throughout elementary school and it was Claire who convinced her to join the cheerleading squad in junior high. They were inseperatable after that. Sandy didn't mind playing second fiddle to Claire's violin. She was happy to be along for the ride. She always felt indebted to Claire.

Throughout all of the turmoil of the last few years, Claire had remained the one constant in her life. Sandy sat there and looked at her friend lying in the hospital bed. Claire was once so full of life and now her rosy skin had turned a pale color of grey. It was hard for Sandy to believe that they were the same age.

Claire's face told a different story. It was only in the last few years that her health had deteriorated. It took everyone by surprise: most of all Sandy.

She let out a big sigh. There was no one around to hear it, but it made Sandy feel better. She was feeling down enough about her situation, without being able to go through it with the support of her best friend.

Claire's eyelid fluttered. Sandy looked up just in time to catch it. Her middle finger on her right hand began to move slowly up and down.

Sandy pulled the sigh back and stood up next to Claire's bed.

Claire's nose twitched.

Her wristed moved.

Sandy took Claire's hand and squeezed. She wanted her best friend to know she was not alone.

She felt Claire's hand squeeze back slightly and she knew Claire was waking up from the sedative.

"I'm here Claire," Sandy said in her softest voice.

Claire's eyelids fluttered again and this time opened slightly. She began to roll her eyes around and found the strength to open them completely.

"Claire," Sandy nearly shouted.

Claire blinked her eyes a few times and finally realized that Sandy was standing in front of her.

"Hi," her friend said back to her, life slowly coming back to her eyes.

22

Before he even had a chance to react, Jeff's head was slammed into the door. He let out a small yelp and Amanda grabbed him by the shoulders. The door jam closed around his neck and pinned him in place.

He felt a rush of pain to his head as the pressure around his neck grew and threatened to crush his windpipe.

"Andrew!" He was able to scream, before the wind was knocked out of him.

Amanda jumped into action. She knew

Andrew was behind all of this, and she wasn't going to let him take Jeff too. Amanda grabbed the door knob and pushed back in the other direction with all of her might. Andrew obviously wasn't expecting this because the door went flying in the other direction, pinning him between it and the wall in the undersized bathroom.

Jeff wasn't expecting it either. All of his concentration was on trying to unpin his head, and when Amanda pushed the door, Jeff went crashing to the ground. He grabbed his throat and began coughing uncontrollably.

Amanda immediately grabbed him by the legs and pulled him out of the doorway.

Jeff propped himself up against the wall and tried to catch his breath.

"Get out of here now Andrew," Amanda demanded. She gripped the ax in her hand and stood between Jeff and the doorway.

Andrew did not respond.

"I have the ax you used to kill Kyle, and if you don't come out now, I'm going to come in there with it," Amanda raged.

"I didn't kill anyone," Andrew finally cried from behind the door.

"There are only three people left in the mausoleum and Jeff or I didn't do it," Amanda reasoned.

"There's someone else in here with us."

"What are you talking about?" Amanda

asked.

"You just came up from the basement, right?" Andrew responded.

"Yes," Amanda simply said.

"That's why I locked myself in here. I heard footsteps coming and you were no were to be found."

"What? Am I expected to believe that?" she asked.

"Yes. Someone tried to get in. I think whoever it was got scared off when they heard you and Jeff coming back up the stairs."

Amanda thought for a second. Was this a trap? Was he trying to get her to drop her defenses so he could attack? She couldn't get another thought out of her head before Jeff interrupted.

"He's right," Jeff said.

She looked down at him. His neck was a bright shade of red, but he didn't seem to have sustained any real damage.

Amanda crouched down next to him and asked, "How do you know?"

"Look at the footprints," Jeff choked.

Amanda looked down at the ground at the bloody footprints. They were all over the room. They led from the basement to the bathroom then back out to the main area of the mausoleum.

"So?" She didn't get it.

"If Andrew locked himself in the

bathroom, how could have bloody footprints go from the bathroom door back out into the mausoleum?"

It was possible that Jeff was right. Amanda tried to think of a way Andrew could have made the footprints and ended up back in the bathroom. That would have required a lot of effort.

"Amanda," Andrew called out. "You know me. You've known me for years. Do you really think I could have done something like kill Kyle?"

The sound of his voice brought Amanda back to her car this morning. She wasn't sure if it was the claustrophobia of being trapped inside the mausoleum or the haziness of her head wound, but she felt now like she was thinking clearer than she had all day.

"Of course you couldn't," she gushed. "I'm sorry. I'm not thinking straight."

The door of the bathroom began to stir and Andrew emerged from behind it clutching the hatchet in his hand. He looked down at Jeff.

"I'm sorry Jeff," he stammered.

Jeff finally caught his breath. "It's okay."

"I thought you were trying to kill me."

"Try a stunt like that again and I might," Jeff blurted.

"So what's the plan," Amanda butted in.

Jeff stood up to join the group.

"We need to find a way out of here, and

we need to stick together," Jeff said.

"We should try the basement," Andrew suggested.

"There's no way out down there. Amanda and I only found offices."

"You don't think we should follow those footsteps and see where they lead?" Amanda asked.

"What?" Andrew said. "So we can be next on the list?"

"We have an ax, hatchet, and a hammer. There are three of us. I'm not really that worried," Amanda stated confidently.

"Forget it," Andrew said. "We need to try the basement again."

"Trust me," Amanda said. "You do not want to go down there."

"Jeff?" Andrew turned to him.

"Amanda, do you really want to go out there?"

"Yes, let's follow the footsteps. That way no one will take us by surprise."

"Okay," Jeff said. "Let's try it."

***

The first footstep on the shiny marble floor of the mausoleum looked different. The blood seemed pinker when contrasted with the pale white marble and the harsh florescent lights.

Jeff let the caravan, hammer in hand, perched near his shoulder. Amanda followed in quick succession, ax gripped firmly at her side. Andrew brought up the rear with the hatchet and kept an eye out behind them as the train moved through the mausoleum.

The footprints led them back to the east side of the mausoleum towards the rubble of the collapsed burial chambers. The prints were very methodical. Who ever was in the building with them walked with a purpose.

They uneventfully made their way to the bottom of the rubble pile. The footsteps climbed the hill of ruins and crested the top.

"Looks like we are climbing," Jeff mouthed.

He carefully took a few steps up the pile, careful to avoid the splintering, rotten wood. Amanda followed quickly behind, and Andrew struggled. He still wasn't seeing quite clearly, although he was beginning to come to his senses. It was tough for him to climb only having use of one hand, and trying to hold the hatchet with it.

Suddenly, Amanda stopped climbing. She looked down into the rubble below her and something caught her eye.

"Jeff," she whispered.

He stopped climbing and turned back around to face her.

"What?" He mouthed back to her.

"The blue prints are down here," she whispered motioning deep into the rubble. "They might tell us another way out."

Jeff mouthed "get them."

Amanda looked down. She could see Jeff's clipboard, but she wasn't sure how she was going to reach it. The broken marble wasn't the issue, the shards of wood were. She took the handle of the ax and drove it straight down into the rubble towards the clipboard.

The wood splintered around it and Amanda began to slowly move the ax in a circular motion. She made the hole in the rubble wider and wider until it was big enough to fit her arm down through it.

Amanda withdrew the ax and laid it by her side. The clipboard was near the bottom of the rubble, nearly two feet away. Amanda laid her body flat against the pile of rubble and slowly pushed her hand down the rabbit hole she had created.

She slowly moved her hand towards the clipboard, careful not to bump her arm against the side of the tunnel. Amanda felt the tips of her fingers touch the clipboard.

"Almost got it," she whispered to no one in particular.

She slid her finger in the metal hole in the spring loaded clip, and slowly withdrew the clipboard from the hole. She sat up and proudly held it in the air.

"What does it say?" Andrew whispered.

Amanda flipped through the pages, carefully studying each and every blue print on the clipboard.

"It says there's an exit in the office," she exclaimed, probably a little louder than she should have.

"There's nothing in the office," Andrew reminded her. "We just came from there."

"Well," Amanda continued. "According to this, that cedar wall shouldn't be there."

"So we need to get behind that?" Andrew asked.

"Yes, let's go" Amanda said.

"What about the footprints?" Jeff asked.

"Forget it," Amanda responded. "Let's get out of this place now."

Jeff looked down at them. They were right. They needed to get out. He looked back up at the crest of the rubble. He was almost there. He wanted to know where the footprints led.

Amanda and Andrew were already off of the rubble pile and ready to go.

"Come on Jeff," Amanda whispered, motioning him off.

Jeff looked again at the crest and finally decided to climb back down the hill.

He didn't see Slate perched on the other side with a hatchet, waiting to surprise the first person over the hill.

23

Amanda swung the ax and created the first chip in the cedar wall. The boards were arranged horizontally and were firmly nailed in place. They tried earlier to pry them off, but with no luck. Amanda was running low on patience and began chopping at the wall as soon as they entered the office. Jeff and Andrew each stood back near the bathroom entrance and watched her swing.

Andrew had offered to do it, but with one injured arm Amanda figured she could do it quicker herself.

She swung the ax again, aiming for the middle board and another chip of wood flew across the small office. The smell of cedar filled the room with each hit and it reminded Amanda of summers at her grandmother's house.

Her parents worked full time jobs to support the family, so when summer hit, Amanda would always spend the days with her grandmother. She lived in a large Victorian house on the east side of New Castle. There were always children out playing in the streets, but Amanda always preferred books to social interaction.

Amanda's grandmother had a great selection of books, from classics all the way up to recent thrillers and romance novels. She kept them in a spare bedroom at the end of a long hallway in a cedar lined closet.

The smell of cedar permeated each book, and Amanda would spend hours choosing one while her grandmother cooked Augustine's pizza for lunch.

A drop of sweat dripped from her forehead into her eye and brought Amanda's thoughts back to reality. She was nearly through one of the cedar planks.

She brought back the ax again and swung with all of her might. She nearly lost her footing as the ax went crashing through the cedar plank, slicing it into two parts.

Jeff ran over and grabbed one piece of the board, while Amanda grabbed the other. They both pulled and the nails that were holding the board in place cried as they were pried from their duties.

The each piece of the board flopped to the ground. Jeff was careful to step over it as rusty nails jutted every few inches out of the board.

"Can you see anything?" Andrew asked.

Jeff and Amanda peered through the hole they had created in the wall, but it was too dark on the other side to make out anything clearly.

"I think I see something," Jeff blurted out, not really knowing what he was looking at.

"It's a door," Amanda exclaimed, making out a door knob. "Stand back," she instructed Jeff.

Jeff took a few steps back to Andrew's side as Amanda again swung the ax into the next board down.

The next board was much easier to get though. Amanda had chopped through it in only a few swings and Jeff again helped her pry it from the wall. The pieces fell next to the first board, rusty nails sticking out from each direction. It almost looked like they were creating two separate beds made of nails.

Jeff returned back to Andrew's side and Amanda easily removed the next two boards. They had created a cubby hole that was about three feet high and five feet wide.

"I'll go in," Jeff said, stepping over to Amanda.

"We'll be right behind you," she said, motioning Andrew over to her side.

Jeff stepped over to the cubby hole and crouched down, keeping the hammer firmly gripped in his hand. He put one hand on the ground to balance and crawled into the space Amanda created.

The other side of the wall was pitch black and surprisingly warm compared to the rest of the mausoleum. He couldn't see anything. He wasn't even sure he saw a door, but Amanda swore that it was there. He put one hand in front of the other and managed to crawl a few feet.

Jeff fought the urge to stand up, not knowing what he was going to be standing into. He noticed some shadows moving behind him, but didn't feel the presence of Amanda or Andrew in the darkness with him.

He suddenly remembered his cell phone. He reached down around his belt and pulled it out. He mashed the keypad with his palm and suddenly the darkness was filled with an ominous blue glowing light.

Jeff looked around. The walls were the same dark shade and material of the office. It definitely looked like someone put up the cedar wall because they didn't want the crew to escape.

He held the phone out in front of him and realized that Amanda was right. There was a door. Above it was a broken exit sign. Jeff breathed a sigh of relief. Amanda had saved them. They were going to be free.

Jeff held the cell phone above him, saw the ceiling, and knew it was safe to stand. He stretched his legs and took a step towards the door when his pant leg got caught on something. He pointed the cell phone down towards the floor and noticed his pants were snagged on something sharp. He bent over to grab it when a sharp pain hit him in the middle of his forehead.

He stood straight again and put his hand to his head. He pulled it away to reveal a small drop of blood on his hand. He held the cell phone up in front of him again and noticed for the first time that the doorway was blocked. Razor wire was strung seeming haphazardly around the room, blocking the way to the door.

Jeff was surprised that he hadn't noticed it before. It was a dark color, not the shiny metal Jeff was used to seeing on top of fences around his construction sites. As he looked around the room, he realized that it wasn't strung as haphazardly as he first thought. Someone was very specific about the way they put it up. It was placed spread out only a few inches apart. It ran from one wall, back to the opposite wall, and then back again.

There were no gaps more than three or

four inches. It was designed to be impossible to squeeze through. Jeff was engrossed at the infrastructure of the razor wire when he heard the commotion behind him. At first, he wasn't sure what it was. He was in the dark, and his mind was playing tricks on him. But, when he heard Amanda yell, "Run," he knew something was happening.

Jeff quickly crouched back down and crawled back to the opening of the cubby hole. He stayed back far enough so that he couldn't be seen, but had a view of what was going on. He could only see from the waist down and he recognized Amanda and Andrew easily, but there was a third person in the room.

Everything seemed to be happening in slow motion. Jeff didn't have time to react, let alone help. Amanda and Andrew were heading towards the bathroom. The third mysterious person was hot on their tail. Jeff noticed their pursuer must have had something raised in the air, because Jeff could only see one arm.

Amanda and Andrew made it to the bathroom and slammed the door behind them. The figure walked over and grabbed the door knob. They were able to get the door locked in time, because the knob did not turn. Jeff saw the figure stand at the door for a moment before turning to face the half demolished cedar wall.

Jeff realized that the figure knew he was there. Whoever had trapped them in here had done it on purpose. His mind raced with options. He was trapped if he stayed behind the cedar wall.

The figure took a few more steps towards Jeff. Jeff watched in horror as the figure's other hand came into view. The figure was carrying a hatchet.

Jeff made the quick decision to run for it. With the hammer gripped tightly in his hand, Jeff quickly crawled out from the cubby hole and bolted toward the door of the office. He didn't even look back to see if the figure was following him, he could tell by the footsteps that someone was close behind him.

He reached the door of the office and escaped into the chilling cold of the burial chambers. He knew the east hallway was collapsed and he wouldn't be able to climb the pile of rubble with someone this close on his tail, so he darted right and ran down the west hallway.

Jeff could hear the footsteps behind him getting closer. He expected to feel the pierce of a hatchet in his back at any second. This fueled him to run faster. His boots slipped on the shiny white marble, but he was able to keep his balance.

He felt the air behind his head break, and he realized that his pursuer was swinging the hatchet as his head. He continued down the west hallway, passing burial chamber after burial chamber, but there was no where to hide. He was quickly approaching the end of the hallway, and it was a dead end. The collapse had taken out all escape routes and he was out of options.

Jeff stopped dead in his tracks, took a deep breath as the footsteps behind him grew in his ears, and turned to face his pursuer. He didn't even get a chance to see his face before the flat side of the hatchet struck him in the side of his head.

Jeff fell to the ground, trying to clutch his head as his vision went white and he quickly lost consciousness.

24

"It's awful quiet out there," Andrew said.

Amanda was only partially listening. She was worried about Jeff. "What do you think happened to Jeff?"

"I don't know," Andrew said. "Everything happened so fast. Did you get a look at his face?"

"No," Amanda stammered. "I just saw someone coming at us with a hatchet. That was all I needed."

Amanda stretched her legs out and returned them into their position. They were sitting with their backs to the door, legs stretched out to the other side of the bathroom propping the door shut.

Andrew found a lock on the door and latched it just in time, but there was no way the flimsy rusted lock on the knob was going to hold anyone out for too long.

"I didn't see him either. All I heard was you yelling and I took off after you."

"We need to go out there and find Jeff," Amanda said. She still clutched the ax in her hand. "We have weapons."

Andrew gripped the hatchet. "Do you really want to get into a fight with him? You saw what he did to Kyle."

"And Simon," her voice trailed off.

Andrew didn't quite know what happened to Simon, but he was sure he didn't want to know the details.

Amanda grew quiet. Her face began to change. "Is it even worth fighting any more? Whoever trapped us in here obviously has it planned so we can't escape."

"You don't know that," Andrew quickly responded. "Maybe Jeff found a way out behind that wall."

"You think he escaped?" Amanda perked up a little.

"Well," Andrew wanted to be optimistic.

"If he did, I'm sure he's getting help right now."

Amanda wasn't filled with the comfort she was hoping Andrew was going to provide. They had both witnessed the same thing. They saw Jeff disappear behind the wall, but before they were able to follow him, someone burst into the room waving a hatchet at them.

"Do you have a bucket list," Amanda asked flatly.

"A bucket list?" Andrew asked, as if she was speaking a different language.

"I thought everyone in the world knew what a bucket list was." She looked him in the eye.

"A movie?" he asked.

"No, a list of things you want to do before you die," Amanda informed him.

"Oh," Andrew thought. "I never really thought much about it before."

"I do."

"Of course you do," Andrew nearly laughed. "You're always so organized and on top of things, it wouldn't surprise me if your entire day was on a list."

Amanda gave him a playful smack on the chest. "Hey! I'm not that organized."

"Please," Andrew howled. "I bet you get up at the same time every morning, to the minute!"

Amanda blushed.

"I knew it," he yelled.

"Shh," Amanda instructed. "Keep your voice down."

"So what's on this bucket list?" Andrew asked in a whisper.

"I want to run a marathon."

"I thought the things on this bucket list were supposed to be fun," Andrew asked.

"That would be fun. I think it would give me a sense of accomplishment. Like, I've been able to finish something."

"What else?"

"I'd like to be able to speak another language."

"Any one in particular?" Andrew asked.

"French, maybe. I'd like to see Paris," Amanda responded. "I took French in high school but I never used it, so I don't remember much."

"Makes sense."

"What about you?" Amanda was curious. "There's got to be something on your list. What is it?"

"I'd like to go rock climbing," Andrew confessed.

"There you go! That's a good one," Amanda quietly cheered. "I want to learn to ski."

"I'd like to own a house."

"I'd like to get married and have children."

"I want to become a millionaire," Andrew

said.

"Good luck with that working here," Amanda chuckled. "I would like to start my own business."

"Doing what?"

"Maybe a bakery. My friends all say I make the best cupcakes."

"I never knew you could bake," Andrew replied.

"Yes," Amanda said. "My grandmother taught me. I used to spend summers at her house and we used to do everything together."

The thought of her grandmother brought Amanda back to the gravity of the situation. She had passed away only a few years ago, but Amanda still thought about her every day. In some ways she was more of a mother to her than her own mother was.

"I'd like to find a boyfriend some day," Andrew confessed.

Amanda sat up straight. "Wait a minute. You're--" she giggled before she could finish her sentence.

"Why is that funny?" He asked.

"I just always assumed, you were--" She stopped. "I just mean you're always so flirty with me and charming."

"And you don't think that can transfer?"

Amanda blushed. "I always--" She couldn't finish what she was saying.

"You always what? Go on. Say it."

She was embarrassed. "I," she hesitated, "always thought you had a crush on me."

"I always thought you had a crush on me!"

Amanda laughed. "No. Well, maybe a little."

Andrew put his arm around her. "You're barking up the wrong tree, but I appreciate the gesture."

Amanda sighed. She looked around the small room. "Is this the last room I'm ever going to see?"

Andrew looked her in the eye. He could see she was grasping at straws.

"No," he said firmly. "We are going to get out of here."

"You know how I feel about Mondays," she said, trying to take a smile.

"This is going to go down in history as the worst Monday of them all."

Amanda looked down. A lock of her golden blonde hair fell, covering her eyes. She pushed it back and Andrew saw the tears form in her eyes.

"I don't know if I can keep fighting if Jeff is dead."

"Jeff is not dead. He got out. He had to have. We just need to hold on in here until he gets back."

Just as Andrew spoke the words, Amanda heard Jeff calling her name from outside the door, "Amanda."

Andrew perked up he when heard Jeff's voice. He backed off of the door. Amanda jerked to her feet, leaving the ax on the ground next to her.

"Jeff," she called out.

Amanda pushed past Andrew and threw open the door to the bathroom.

Jeff was standing near the entrance to the office. He stood in an awkward position and his hands behind his back. His head was wounded and blood ran from a fresh wound just above his left eyebrow.

Amanda smiled as she saw him.

"You're alive," she screamed.

His face was not happy to see her. He frowned and grimaced when he should have been smiling.

Amanda took another step away from the bathroom door towards Jeff.

"Are you okay?" She asked.

Jeff didn't respond. Amanda noticed his eyes were red and bloodshot and he looked like he was about to cry at any minute.

"Jeff?" she asked again. "What's wrong? Did you find a way out?"

Jeff's eyes grew wide and Amanda took it as a warning to stop moving. Jeff discreetly shook his head no and motioned with his eyes to Amanda's right.

Amanda was only a few steps out of the

bathroom. She couldn't feel Andrew behind her, but she knew he couldn't have gone far. Amanda, keeping her head very still, focused her eyes as far to the right as she could.

She didn't see anything.

"Jeff?" She warily said, starting to get worried.

Jeff mouthed something but she was unable to hear him.

"What?" She asked him to repeat.

He mouthed it again, only this time, Amanda was able to make out the words.

"I'm sorry," he said.

Before Amanda had a chance to figure out what he was sorry for, a blinding pain hit her on the right side of her head. She crumbled to the ground and clutched the side of her head. She felt a warm rush of sticky heat and pulled her hand away to reveal it was covered in crimson red death.

Amanda looked up to see who hit her, but the gushing blood ran into her eyes, causing a red haze to blur her vision. She looked back to Jeff. Even though her rose colored vision, she could see him starting to cry.

She realized what he was sorry for. It was a trap. The killer had used Jeff to lure her out.

Amanda pushed her hand back to the side of her head in an effort to stop the throbbing pain that was becoming more noticeable by the second.

Andrew stood behind Amanda in the doorway of the bathroom watching the entire scene unfold. He saw a hatchet come down and clock Amanda in the side of the head. He saw the skin covering her skull pull away as the hatchet tore through it, eventually hitting the bone.

He saw Amanda fall to the ground in pain and the puddle of blood beneath her begin to grow. He was scared and a coward. Andrew pulled the door of the bathroom shut and flipped the rusty lock to provide some protection.

He left Amanda and Jeff out there to die.

25

Andrew stood behind the door in shock. He couldn't believe that he abandoned Amanda the way he did. She was bleeding and she needed his help, but there was nothing he could do except hide.

He looked the door up and down. He noticed for the first time that the door opened out. He and Amanda had been sitting there no more than a few minutes ago with their backs to the door. The killer could have easily pulled the door open. The lock was not strong enough to provide much protection.

Andrew heard some commotion outside the door. He heard Jeff mumble something, but couldn't make it out. He then heard what sounded like furniture being moved across the floor.

He took a deep breath and again looked the door up and down. He couldn't stay hidden inside this bathroom forever. He noticed that his hatchet and Amanda's ax were both lying on the floor of the bathroom.

Andrew quickly changed his mind. He had two options. He could stay in here and be a victim, or he could go out there and attempt to be a hero. He grabbed the ax off of the floor and gripped it tightly in his right hand. He had to do something to save Amanda.

He flicked the rusty lock open and grabbed the door knob. The ax handle was hurting his hand he was gripping it so tightly. Andrew turned the knob quickly, knowing he would lose his nerve if he didn't open the door quickly. He pushed. Nothing happened. He pushed again, this time using his foot for extra leverage, but the door wouldn't budge.

Something was blocking it.

Andrew pushed again, but whatever it was wasn't giving an inch.

He looked down in his hand at the ax. Whoever locked him in here wanted him in here for a reason, and Andrew wasn't about to make it any easier for the killer. He was not going to go down without a fight. He wasn't going to be depressed like Amanda was, he was going to fight.

Andrew lifted the ax above his head and brought it down square in the middle of the door. He was going to chop his way out.

***

Jeff struggled to free himself from the ropes binding his hands. Slate had chased him down the row of burial chambers and knocked him out near the end. When he woke up, he was back in the office. Slate was standing over him, demanding that he call Amanda's name. If he refused, Slate threatened to kill him instead.

He never thought he would do it. Sacrifice another life for his. He didn't really have time to think it through with the hatchet blade pressed against his throat.

Jeff pulled his arms like a contortionist trying to get free. He kept one eye on what Slate was doing, but he didn't comprehend what was going on.

Amanda laid on the ground, still clutching her head, desperately trying to stop the bleeding. Slate violently grabbed her and threw her against the door of the bathroom. Amanda yelped in pain, and held her head. It was nearly impossible to see anything through the blurry crimson haze.

Slate pushed past Jeff and grabbed the side of the sturdy wooden desk. With a solid push the desk was in motion heading straight for Amanda. She didn't notice what was happening until the desk was upon her.

Jeff still struggled to get loose and make sense in his mind what Slate was doing. The ropes were binding his hands firmly behind his back. Every pull burned them deeper into his skin, but his thoughts were so focused on getting free that he was unable to feel it.

The desk slid to a stop right in front of Amanda. She looked up and noticed the flat wood surface in front of her face. Slate moved around the desk, opposite of Amanda, and gave the desk one final push.

It slammed Amanda's head into the door of the bathroom. She let out a yelp as she found herself pinned to the door. Slate let out a sound that was somewhere between a laugh and a cough.

The desk had also pushed Jeff's cell phone across the floor next to Amanda. Jeff saw it light up from across the room and looked down at his belt. Somehow he must have dropped it while trying to run away from Slate.

The first ax slam startled Jeff. It came though the door just inches above Amanda's head.

Amanda let out a yelp. She couldn't see what was going on, but she knew something was happening. Her left arm was wedged behind her back, but she maneuvered her right hand and tried to push the desk away from her.

Slate stood on the other side and pushed back. There was no way Slate was going to let Amanda free.

The ax disappeared from its newly created hole and Jeff imagined Andrew was pulling it back again inside for another swing.

Jeff let out a scream, "Andrew! Stop"

Slate quickly let go of the desk and ran over to Jeff, and held the hatchet to his throat. "Shut up."

Jeff fell silent.

With Slate no longer on the other side of the desk, Amanda once again pushed the desk with her right hand and was able to move it a few inches. She pulled her head away from the door just as the ax crashed through it again.

If Jeff hadn't distracted Slate, the ax would have hit Amanda in the shoulders.

Amanda leveraged her left arm, which she freed from behind her back, and braced herself for another push of the desk.

The ax retreated back into the bathroom.

Jeff let out a chuckle.

"Shit," Slate exclaimed.

Jeff was proud that they were able to back Slate into a corner. There was no way Slate could hold the desk and keep Jeff quiet at the same time.

Slate released the hatchet from Jeff's neck and darted back over to the desk. Slate grabbed the corner of the desk and slammed it back towards Amanda.

Amanda's right arm fell to her side, but her left was pinned between the door and the desk, parallel to the floor. Amanda attempted to push back. Her left arm was weaker than her right, but she still had strength left in it.

Her elbow moved slightly away from door as she pushed with her hand against the desk.

Slate felt the desk give way and pushed back hard. The push caught Amanda by surprise. Her elbow slammed against the door and her wrist began to move backwards as the edge of the desk attempted to push towards her.

Amanda felt her wrist bending back further than she could handle. The tension was too much. Slate gave the desk another hard push, and Amanda felt the sharp pain as her wrist snapped.

She let out a scream. Jeff couldn't tell if it was the sound of Amanda's wrist snapping or the sound of the ax once again crashing through the door. It landed directly next to Amanda's head. If she had been another inch or two to the left, she wouldn't have been so lucky.

Jeff needed to take the pressure off of

Amanda. He again yelled for Andrew, "Hey, stop!"

Slate once again ran from the desk over to Jeff. Slate held the hatchet to Jeff's neck.

"Shut up," Slate once again firmly warned.

This gave Amanda a brief reprieve. She lifted her right arm and pushed the desk away slightly. This allowed her left arm to drop into her lap. She screamed again as her wrist fell onto her leg.

She looked down and saw it through the blood haze. It was bent back at a 45 degree angle. The skin was torn and there was a bone protruding from the bottom of her wrist.

Amanda let out another yelp and her eyes watered. This helped clear some of the blood from her eyes. She couldn't let this stop her. She reached up again with her right hand and braced it against the side of the desk. She took a deep breath and gave it a push. It slid a few inches away from her.

"Amanda," Jeff croaked.

Slate had had enough. "I told you to shut up."

Slate took the blade of the hatchet and slid it along the left side of Jeff's throat. Slate pushed just hard enough to slice into Jeff's throat, but not enough to sever his artery.

Jeff let out another yelp and pushed away. Slate let him drop to the ground and bolted back over to the desk.

Amanda saw Slate coming. She wanted to give the desk another push, but her strength was quickly draining.

Slate grabbed the desk and gave it another hard push. The desk slammed back into Amanda, this time trapping her head and shoulders firmly between the desk and the door.

Jeff again attempted to scream to stop Andrew from swinging the ax, but the slice to his neck wouldn't allow another louder than a whisper.

"Andrew," he croaked. His voice was failing him.

The ax came crashing through the door again. This time, again to Amanda's right, creating a sizeable hole through the bottom half of the door. Amanda yelped again, but her voice was muffled by the wood of the desk. The ax again retreated back into the bathroom.

Slate pushed harder. The air in Amanda's lungs began to leak out through her nose creating bubbles through the blood. She tried to breathe in again but her lungs were being crushed by the desk. She gasped for what little oxygen she could take in, but it wasn't enough to breathe.

Amanda tried to speak, but couldn't.

The ax again came crashing through the door again. The sound was different this time. The crash happened and there was a spitting sound. Jeff looked up and saw what had happened.

Slate looked across the desk.

The ax crashed through the door and hit Amanda directly in the back of the head. Her eyes fluttered and closed one final time.

26

Andrew stopped with the ax still stuck in the door. This hit felt different. With every hit before, the ax bounced. This time the blade found something solid. He was confident he just hit whatever was blocking the door.

He gripped the handle of the ax and yanked it free from the door. The blade was covered in blood.

Andrew nearly dropped it. He was shocked with what he saw. He quickly dropped to the floor and looked out the hole he made with a prior swing.

He couldn't see much of anything. He saw that a desk had been pushed up against the door, but couldn't see the reason why his ax may have drawn blood. He did notice Jeff's cell phone lying on the ground just below the hole.

Andrew contemplated reaching his hand out to grab it. He listened closely outside the door and heard some movement. He made a quick decision to go for it and quickly pushed his hand through the hole in the door.

His hand quickly found the cold floor and he searched for the phone. He flopped his hand left and right and his fingers quickly found it. He grabbed it and pulled his hand back inside just missing the sharp jagged wood of the door.

Andrew slid the phone into his pocket.

He still wanted out of the bathroom. He quickly ruled out swinging at the door with the ax again. He didn't know why there was blood on the blade, but he didn't want to risk doing any more damage.

Andrew figured he had weakened enough to try again.

He positioned himself against the back wall of the bathroom. It was only a few feet from the door, but he wanted to give himself a running start.

Andrew pushed off from the wall and flew towards the door. He hit it with his good shoulder and the door gave way. He crashed through it and the wood, which once seemed so solid, went crashing down all around him.

He expected to fall to the ground but he landed hard on the desk. A piece of the door hit him in the head and he curled into the fetal position to avoid any injury.

Andrew brushed off a piece of wood from his mid section and it fell to the floor. He quickly looked around the room and saw Jeff being pulled out of the room by his leg. He couldn't get a clear look at who was pulling him.

"Jeff," he screamed out.

Jeff looked up and made eye contact with Andrew just as the final pull drug him out into the cold burial chamber room.

Andrew propped himself up on the desk and came face to face with the reason the ax had blood on it.

Amanda.

She was pinned between the desk and what was left of the door. Her head had been split open from the back.

Andrew was sick. He had done this. Before he could control it, he felt a sudden wave of nausea overtake him. There was a tickle in the back of his throat, and before he knew it bile was pouring out of his mouth.

He hadn't eaten anything all day and the vomit stung his throat as it came up. His abdomen convulsed and the air left his lungs.

Andrew tried to catch is breath as bile dripped from his mouth and nose. He looked again over at Amanda and another wave hit him.

He dropped off of the desk to the floor and smashed into his injured shoulder. He screamed in pain and rolled over to his back. He turned his head and coughed up the remaining bile, using his sleeve to wipe his mouth.

It was down to him and Jeff. He had to continue fighting.

He reached down into his pocket and pulled out Jeff's phone. His eyes stung as they filled with tears and he dialed the first number in the call history.

It was Sandy's phone.

He held it to his ear and listen to it as it began to ring.

27

Sandy didn't realize how long she had been at the hospital. She looked down at the clock on her dashboard and it said 6:50. She had 10 minutes to make it across town or she was going to be late.

She put the car in reverse and pulled out of her parking spot at the hospital. She threw it in drive as her cell phone began to ring. She reached for her purse which she had thrown on the passenger's seat.

Sandy dug through it looking for the ringing cell phone. Her hand found her wallet first. She pushed it aside and dug deeper into the bag. She found a pack of tissues, her make up case, and her checkbook, but she couldn't locate her phone.

She took her eyes off of the road and glanced down at her bag. She wasn't able to see into it so she opened it up and glanced back at the road. There were no obstacles in her way so she looked back down at her bag.

It was now wide open. She rifled through the mess as the cell phone continued to ring, but she couldn't find it.

She glanced back up at the road and noticed she was drifting into oncoming traffic. She jerked the wheel to the right and centered herself back in her lane.

The phone continued to ring.

She pulled her hand out of her bag and placed it back on the wheel. She wasn't going to risk an accident to answer the phone. Whoever it was could wait until she stopped.

The phone stopped ringing.

Sandy looked down at the clock. 6:54. She just might make it.

The phone started ringing again.

"Seriously?" Sandy screamed out loud.

Sandy reached for her purse again. This time she forcefully thrust her hand into her purse, hell bent on finding the phone.

She found it with no problems this time and pulled it out. She looked down at the phone.

"Oh, for god's sake" she said aloud. It was Jeff's number on the caller id.

She pushed the green button and held the phone to her ear.

"Jeff, I'm running late, this had better be good," she said sternly into the phone.

She listened for a minute. She made a few noises to acknowledge she was listening.

Sandy glanced down at the clock. 6:57.

She propped the phone between her ear and her shoulder and turned on her left turn signal. She waited for a few cars to pass and pulled into a parking lot. She found a space and pulled into it.

"Yes," Sandy said into the phone.

She turned the ignition and pulled out the key. In the reflection of the car window, she could see a large white building. It towered over her car and she had a hard time seeing the top of it.

Sandy glanced around the parking lot and noticed there were only a few other cars in the lot with her.

"Yes," she said again into the phone. The person on the other side of the call was dominating the conversation.

Sandy grabbed her purse and hopped out of the car. She slammed the door shut and walked toward the towering white building.

She stopped just before she got to the entrance.

"Yes," she said into the phone. "Everything is all set for tomorrow, Jeff. Don't worry. Be there at 7 a.m. sharp. I gotta go, I'm running late."

Sandy hung up the phone and dropped it into her purse. She looked up at the steeple on top of the building and opened the front door. She hated to be late for Sunday church service.

28

Andrew held the phone to his ear. It continued to ring. Four rings. Five rings. Finally, he got Sandy's voicemail.

"Hi you've reached Sandy Slate. I can't take your call right now."

Andrew hung up the phone.

"Fuck this," he said aloud to no one. "I'm calling the cops."

Andrew dialed 9-1-1 on the phone and held it to his ear.

Before it had a chance to ring, Andrew heard a gurgling coming from the burial chambers. It was Jeff.

Ring.

He carefully crept over to the door, keeping a firm grip on the phone.

Ring.

Another gurgle echoed throughout the mausoleum. "Stop," he heard Jeff whisper.

Andrew wanted to help him. He took a step outside of the office into the burial chamber room. He listened again to figure out which aisle Jeff was in.

Ring.

Andrew heard another voice. He couldn't quite make out what it was saying, but it sounded like the voice and Jeff were having a conversation in between Jeff's croaks.

He took another step into the burial chamber room. He realized that the voices were coming from the west side of the mausoleum.

Andrew quietly walked over to the row of burial chambers and stuck his head around the corner. He could see Jeff tied up, arms behind his back, backed into a row of burial chambers.

There was someone standing over him, but the figure's back was turned to block Andrew's view.

"This is the 911 dispatcher. What is your emergency?" A voice from the phone flatly stated.

Andrew took a breath in to speak, but quickly realized that if he spoke now, the figure and Jeff would be able to hear every word. He would give up his advantage of being unseen.

"This is the 911 dispatcher. Is anyone there?"

He took a step back. He had a decision to make. He could either talk to the dispatcher and ask for help or he could help Jeff.

"Hello?" The voice on the phone said, growing impatient.

Andrew quietly took a few steps back. When he was sure he was out of sight, he dashed back into the office. There was no reason he couldn't do both. He was going to call for help and help Jeff.

"Hello. My name is Andrew Evans. I am an employee of Crane Construction. We were hired to demolish the old mausoleum on Old Pittsburgh Road and there's been an accident."

"What kind of accident?" The dispatcher asked.

"Part of the ceiling collapsed and we are trapped inside."

"Is anyone injured?"

"Well, that's the other thing. There's also a killer in the building. So far there are at least four victims."

"Sir," the dispatcher said. "I don't know if this is a prank or not, but I am sending out a unit to the mausoleum."

"Good," Andrew responded. "This is no joke. Now, hurry!"

Andrew hung up the phone and slid it into his pocket. He took a deep breath and gave himself a minute to think. He needed a weapon.

It made him sick to his stomach to think about it, but he needed the ax. He glanced over at the desk and saw Amanda again. He resisted the urge to bend over and wretch and quickly pushed his eyes away.

He looked past the desk into the bathroom. He saw the ax laying on the floor next to the hatchet.

Andrew climbed up onto the top of the desk. Amanda's blood had formed a thin sticky layer over the top of the desk. Andrew used his good arm to prop himself up, and fully laid himself out on the desk.

His head and shoulders stuck out over the desk and through the broken door into the bathroom. He positioned himself so that his good arm could reach above his head and he reached into the bathroom searching for the handle of the ax.

He found the handle of the hatchet first. He grabbed it and flopped it on the desk next to him. He reached back into the bathroom, swiping his hand from left to right until he found the handle of the ax. He pulled it out of the bathroom and hopped off the desk.

Andrew grabbed the hatchet and tucked

it in the back of his pants, and gripped the ax by its handle. He walked, firmly, out into the burial chamber room.

The air outside the office had a different smell. The chill in the air reminded Andrew of a meat locker. His grandfather was a butcher and it always scared him when his mother used to make him visit his grandfather at work.

He paused briefly behind the row of burial chambers before stepping out into the aisle. He let the ax fall to his side and took a stance about 20 feet away from Jeff and the figure.

The figure was hunched over Jeff and Andrew couldn't tell what they were doing.

"Let him go," Andrew demanded.

The figure stood up to face him. He recognized the face.

"Slate?" he asked.

"I hate it when people call me by my last name," Sandy said to him.

"What the hell are you doing here?"

"I could ask you the same question. You're not supposed to be here."

"Amanda--" Andrew trailed off. Just saying her name brought the bile to the back of his throat.

"I only called four people for this job. Four specific people. You shouldn't have come."

Andrew glanced down at Jeff. He was bloody, but alive.

"Why are you doing this?" Andrew demanded to know.

Jeff croaked something. Sandy looked down at him. "What's that Jeff?" She asked, giving him a swift kick in the leg.

He repeated himself, but he was too far away from Andrew to be heard.

"What did he say?" Andrew asked Sandy.

"He said," she stared Andrew in the eye. "The accident."

29

Seven Months Prior

The day started off like any other. The sun was shining bright. Amanda was early as usual. The rest of the crew wandered in at their own pace. They knew this made Eddie angry, but there was no way he could motivate them to get in any earlier than seven.

It was two weeks into the job. Today was an important day because they had to install several metal poles all around the property. Each man had a specific job. Lyle and Kyle were on the ground. They were in charge of guiding each pole into the correct hole. Simon was in charge of the pile driver.

The machine itself was huge; nearly a story high. Simon's job was to move the pole into place with the crane and then set the pile driver. Lyle and Kyle were to guide the pole into the hole and move back. Simon then charged up the pile driver and began driving it into the ground. Amanda was in charge of safety. Eddie always insisted that there be an extra person around just to keep an eye out for anything unusual.

Amanda was good at that. She liked that position. It gave her a sense of importance on a job site. She felt like she was in charge.

Jeff showed up that morning, late as usual. By the time he got there, the crew already had one pole in the ground. Eddie walked up to Jeff just as he was getting out of his car.

"Hey man," Eddie said, extending his hand.

Jeff juggled his lunch pail in one hand and put his car keys away with his other. Quickly letting his keys fall into his pocket, he grabbed Eddie's hand and shook it firmly.

"How's it going? Are the poles in the ground yet?" Jeff asked.

"Give it time. Give it time. These things

don't come quickly," Eddie said trying to keep his patience. Jeff really had no idea of the time and effort these things took, but since the jobs started rolling in at a slower pace, Jeff had no choice but to get back to being more hands on.

They began to walk towards the site.

"So," Jeff asked, "how'd she like it?"

"Oh, man, it was great. I had no idea she'd go so crazy."

"Oh yeah, women love that shit. All romance and shit."

Eddie had taken Sandy out for a night on the town for their anniversary. It had been a while since they had spent much time together. Since Jeff's business hit a rough patch, Eddie was forced to put more and more time in on each job to help Jeff keep costs down. He knew that Sandy resented the situation a bit, but Eddie was more than happy to pitch in for Jeff. After all, if it wasn't for him he wouldn't have met his beautiful wife or been able to give her the life they shared together.

"Thanks again for letting me take the day off yesterday. How'd you survive without me?" Eddie was curious to hear the answer.

"It was fine. Really. Not a bit of trouble."

They had reached the crew. Eddie looked up just in time to see Amanda. She was walking their way.

"Good morning Jeff," she said wiping sweat from her brow. Her blonde hair glistened in the morning sun.

"How's it going Amanda? We ready for another post in the ground?" Jeff asked her.

"We sure are, Lyle and Kyle are over there right now ready for Simon to drop it in." As soon as Amanda said it, she turned to make sure it was true. They had been in no mood for working this morning and the brothers were grating on Amanda's nerves. Amanda hoped for the best but she only saw one brother, Lyle.

"Where the hell is Kyle," Eddie asked.

Amanda spun back around to look Eddie in the eyes, "I don't know. He was here just a minute ago." She let out a grunt, twirled around, and stormed off towards where Lyle was standing.

She approached him with vigor. "Where the hell did your brother go?" she demanded.

"Him and Simon are at it again," Lyle said, pointing towards Simon in the crane.

Amanda noticed Simon moving the pile driver over to begin pounding the giant pole they had just placed into the ground. But Kyle was still no where to be seen.

Jeff and Eddie walked over and stopped behind Amanda. The four of them stood around the giant black pole that was sticking out of the ground. They all turned to face each other at almost the exact same time. Jeff and Eddie had their backs to a large stack of plywood that had been delivered the day before and Amanda and

Lyle had their backs towards the crane, not noticing the pile driver was slowly moving their way.

"What is going on here?" Eddie said, somewhere between authoritative and concerned.

"Simon and Kyle were talking shit about each other again on the walkie talkie. You know how it is with those two. Simon's a douche. He thinks he knows everything and Kyle can't let anything go," Lyle explained. "He stormed off somewhere. I can't keep track of him."

If the group wasn't so engrossed in Lyle's story they would have noticed Kyle behind them climbing up the side of the crane. Simon was wearing his ear protection so it even took him by surprise when Kyle swung open the door of the crane and tried to push his way inside.

"What is your problem, man," Kyle snarled.

"What? You think you can take me?" Simon responded in typical *quién-es-mas-macho* fashion.

"You're such a douchebag Simon, I could kick your ass with one arm tied behind my back," Kyle said, clenching his fists.

"Go ahead pussy. Punch me. You'll be dead before you even hit the ground."

"You're all talk, if you want to fight me, go ahead and do it," Kyle said.

Simon raged. His eyes turned to steel and

Kyle thought for sure that steam was going to come out of his ears like in an old cartoon.

"Talk?" Simon screamed at him. "I'll show you talk!" Simon clenched his fist and slammed it into Kyle's chest.

Kyle nearly lost his balance on the side of the crane, but managed to hold on to the open door. Kyle could no longer control his rage. He let his fist fly and hit Simon squarely in the jaw before he was even able to block it.

A thick line of blood flew from Simon's jaw and spashed across the glass that encased the crane. Simon got his bearings after a moment and spit into his hand. A piece of white sparkled in his hand. Kyle had knocked a tooth loose. Simon didn't even feel the next punch as it was coming down directly on his forehead. It hit him straight between the eyes and his vision blurred.

He couldn't see as he just started swinging. A few punches hit Kyle in the sides but none were able to stop the pummeling that Simon was getting. Again and again Kyle's fists came down on Simon's head. Each one felt to Simon like he was being hit with a sledgehammer. He wasn't a weak man, but Kyle was getting the better of him.

He had to put a stop to it. Simon reached out and grabbed Kyle in a bear hug. He pushed him back with all his might. Kyle's head smashed into the glass, shattering it all over the pair. A shard of glass lodged itself in the back of Kyle's ear. Blood gushed from the gaping wound as the glass tore off a piece of skin on Kyle's head.

He screamed and grabbed for the back of his head. In the process, he hit the shard of glass, driving it deeper into his ear. By this time the shard had pierced a hole in his ear and protruded straight through the cartilage before getting lodged in his fleshy earlobe.

Simon used this opportunity to dive on top of Kyle. The force of their bodies rocking shook the entire crane. Kyle's back landed square in the middle of the crane's control panel. The crane began to move and the heavy pile driver that was attached to it began to sway. Simon felt the crane move and tried to jump off of Kyle. But, it was too late. The pile driver was already in motion. Simon couldn't stop it from moving.

Kyle continued to grab at Simon as Simon reached up for emergency stop on the crane. Kyle, still not realizing what was going on, grabbed up and dug his nails deep into Simon's wrist. Simon screamed as Kyle's nail tore into the ligament in Simon's wrist. Blood gushed from the resulting wound.

Simon grabbed his wrist as it involuntarily twitched from the trauma. He screamed at Kyle.

"What the hell, man? You're gonna kill us

both."

The crane continued to rock. The pile driver swung like a pendulum. Down on the ground the entire team was screaming for the idiots to stop fighting.

"Simon!" Amanda screamed in vain. They were too far away to hear her.

Lyle grabbed his walkie talkie and screamed into it, "stop that thing from swinging. You're gonna hurt someone."

The crane began to slowly rock side to side. Amanda shrieked in horror as she watched. It was going to tip. The weight of the pile driver rocking back and forth was more than the crane could handle.

Jeff began to run towards the crane. He thought for a moment there might be something he'd be able to do. Lyle ran after him and grabbed him by the arm.

"What do you think you're doing, you can't stop that machine."

Everything was happening so quickly. None of the time had time to properly react.

Inside, Kyle and Simon were trying to brace themselves. Simon managed to wedge himself between the seat and the back wall of crane. Kyle struggled. He tried to put both hands out and uses his strength to hold him in place, but his hands kept sliding down the walls. The thick blood the covered them was acting as a lubricant.

The crane teetered back and forth. With each swing Kyle felt his stomach drop. He remembered the feeling from when he was a kid. His parents used to take him and his brother to the amusement park. His favorite rides were always the one that gave him a knot in his stomach. He lived on the adrenaline rush it gave him. But, this feeling was different. There was no fun in the stomach knot knowing it could be the last thing he ever felt.

Simon let out a yelp to get Kyle's attention. In the back of his mind he heard the rest of the crew yelling, but it didn't register in his mind at the time. He was focused on one thing only. Surviving the inevitable: the crane was about to tip over with both of them inside. Simon reached out for Kyle. He was still trying to brace himself when he noticed Simon reaching for him. He reached out and locked onto Simon's hand. The blood felt cold and sticky on Simon's hand. It was almost as if it was acting like glue and holding them together.

One final swing to the right as Simon looked directly into Kyle's eyes as they realized that this was the final swing. The crane swung hard to the left. Only this time there was no going back. It teetered on its side for what seemed like hours before finally crashing to the ground.

The rest of the crew stood on the ground in shock. Amanda held her breath for what seemed like hours as the crane swung back and forth. The entire world came to an end for a minute just before the crane fell. Amanda wasn't sure it was going to start again. Somewhere in her mind she didn't want it to start again. Because she was sure that neither Kyle nor Simon were going to survive the crash.

She watched as the crane crashed down on its left side and landed with a smash not heard by her before or since. The earth beneath the crane gave way and formed a cloud of dust and grime as thick as the night sky. Amanda began running towards the crash before the smoke had cleared. She bumped into Jeff on the way, but caught her balance and kept running. She was sure she saw a flash of Lyle's face in the dust cloud as well.

"Kyle," she screamed, hoping to hear something. It seemed to be her only sense that was working correctly.

She heard Lyle screaming in sheer terror, looking for his brother.

The dust was slowly starting to clear. For the first time she saw the mangled crane clearly. It was a mass of twisted yellow metal. There were shards of glass and metal laying all over the construction site. She saw a hand reaching out. She ran over to it. She grabbed it and pulled as hard as she could.

She had all the proper first aid training. She knew you should never touch an injured person. She might have done more harm then good. But, she didn't care. She had to get whoever it was out of there.

Emerging from the wreckage, she realized that she was pulling on Simon's hand. He was okay. No, he was alive, at least. She pulled harder, bending her legs at the knee and using her entire body. His arm was all bloody but she was able to pull him free from the wreckage. He stumbled to the ground and she gave him a quick once over. He looked okay. He was bloody and dirty. No broken bones that she could see. No major puncture wounds. He was lucky.

"Are you okay?" she asked him.

Simon clutched his side. "Oh shit Amanda. Did you see that?"

He sounded like he just got done watching one of those *When Nature Attacks* shows.

"Can you breathe okay? Can you stand up?"

Simon closed his eyes and took a few deep breaths. He nodded at her. He was okay. He grabbed on to her hand and pulled himself up. He was able to stand. Nothing felt terrible, but nothing felt good either.

Amanda was so happy to see him alive she hugged him. He looked shocked for a minute. She came back to reality and looked around to see where everyone else was. Jeff and

Lyle were standing with someone else. She couldn't make it out through the dust. She ran in their direction as Simon hobbled along behind her.

The closer she got the clearer she could make out the figure. She knew him just by his posture. It was Kyle. She could see the side of his face all bloody. But, he was standing. He was alive too. She smiled to herself as she approached them.

"Are you okay?" she asked him.

"Yeah, I think so," Kyle responded.

Just as Simon approached she said, "You are two of the luckiest bastards I've ever met."

Kyle chuckled.

Something still wasn't right. She wasn't totally comfortable with the situation. She did a quick head count. Someone was missing. Jeff. Lyle. Simon. Kyle. But, Eddie. Where was Eddie? Surely he had run over with the rest of the group.

In the moment before she could turn around to look for her, it dawned on her that she had been hearing this thumping noise throughout the entire ordeal. Thump pound. Thump pound. She had blocked it out. The sound was familiar. She had heard it before. Thump pound. She searched through the inventory of her brain. Thump pound.

A scream from one of the guys pierced through her brain. Thump pound. It lodged in the back of hear head unleashing her hidden memory. Thump pound. The sound was the pile driver.

The scream came from Jeff. She turned to find Eddie lodged against the stack of plywood. The pile driver had fallen from sky and landed on its side. It hit Eddie square in the chest and pinned him against the pile of wood. It was still in motion, each thump pound hitting Eddie squarely in the chest. Blood sprayed across his face with each hit. His skin was a dull grey color. His blood glistened in the morning sun.

30

"So you set this whole thing up?" Andrew asked.

"Yes," Sandy responded. "for Eddie."

"Look, I wasn't there, and I don't know exactly what happened, but it was an accident. No one on the crew meant to kill your husband."

Jeff nodded from the ground, agreeing with Andrew.

"It doesn't matter if they did it on purpose or not, he's still gone. I've lost my husband, I've lost the only job I've ever known, my best friend is dying. Do you need me to go on?"

"Sandy, I'm sorry. Bad things happen to good people," Andrew said, trying to reason with her.

"Oh, blah blah blah. Don't give me the speech. I've had so many people give me the speech over the last seven months, I can recite it by heart."

"This wasn't Jeff's fault. Just let us go and we can forget all about this." He wasn't sure what else to say. No matter how good it sounded in his head, it was all sounding like a big cliché by the time it left his mouth.

Sandy crouched down by Jeff and held the blade of the hatchet to his throat. "Forget it," she said. "I'm not letting him go. And I can't let you go now that you know who did this."

Jeff's eyes grew wide and Andrew took a step towards them.

"Back the fuck up," Sandy yelled at him, pressing the blade into Jeff's neck. A thin spout of blood trickled down his neck into his shirt collar. He squirmed but he wasn't able to move with his hands bound behind his back.

Andrew stopped moving, but firmly gripped the ax.

"Now," Sandy instructed, "drop the ax."

"No," Andrew stood firm.

"Drop it now or I will slice his throat."

"Go ahead. If you hurt him I will kill you. Either way I come out the winner in this fight."

Andrew was bluffing. He had no idea if he had it in him to kill someone, but he wasn't going down without a fight.

Sandy didn't know either to believe him or not, but she wasn't about to take any chances.

"Please," Jeff whispered. "I don't care about me, but let Andrew go."

"What do you mean you don't care about you? That would probably be the first selfless thing you've done in your life. All you care about is yourself."

"What are you talking about?" Jeff asked.

"You ran this business into the ground. You were never around to supervise. The jobs got sloppier and sloppier and the business stopped coming."

"We are in a recession," he exclaimed. "That's the reason that business stopped coming."

"Oh please Jeff," she said. "Take your head out of your ass. That didn't stop Wider Construction from making more money last year than they ever have. You have a reputation around town. You do as little as you can to get by and that's finally caught up with you."

"Sandy," Jeff pleaded.

"You and this sorry excuse for a crew is the reason that Eddie is dead. You're the reason I can no longer support myself. You're the reason my life is ruined."

Tears formed in Sandy's eyes and she screamed at Andrew, "drop the fucking ax."

Andrew was startled and dropped the ax in front of him.

"Now slide it over to me," she instructed.

Andrew hesitated, but kicked the ax towards Sandy and it came to a rest a few inches away from Jeff's leg.

She turned her attention back to Jeff.

"It's okay Sandy," he said to her. "I understand now."

"That was quick," she snarked.

"I don't have anything left either," he admitted. "Neither of us know who we are without this place. I've been fighting it for the last few years, but its over. I knew the moment I had to let you go that it was over. There's no way I'm going to be able to keep this business going without you."

These were the words she was waiting to hear. "Was it worth it?"

"Was what worth it?" Jeff began to cough. The hatchet blade was pushing into his neck so deep that it was difficult to breath.

"Running your business into the ground," she replied.

"Maybe I'm not cut out to run a business," Jeff admitted. "I accept that now."

Sandy was shocked. This was not the way she was expecting this conversation to go.

Andrew took another step forward. This put Sandy on edge.

"Don't take another step," she choked back.

Sandy pushed the hatchet at Jeff's neck and he began to choke uncontrollably.

Andrew knew he had to do something.

"Sandy," he pleaded. "Please stop." More clichés.

"It's too late Jeff. It doesn't matter what you say now," Sandy sobbed. She released her grip slightly on the hatchet and gave Jeff a chance to breath. The blade was still cutting into his neck, but not into his windpipe.

"Was this job even real?" Andrew screamed, trying to distract her from Jeff.

Sandy looked up at him. "Of course it wasn't. I've been planning this entire thing for weeks. Do you really think that row of burial chambers just collapsed? I was rigged it to explode. I couldn't have planned it any better either. Who knew that Lyle would be in there when I did it?"

Sandy turned her focus back to Jeff. She looked him in the eye. His eyes darted away. Sandy felt like she was back in the office on her final day of work.

"Look at me, Jeff," she said calmly.

He didn't.

"Look at me, Jeff," she said again, her voice rising at the end.

She loosened the grip the hatchet blade even more so that Jeff was easily able to move his head.

He looked up and met her eyes.

"I'm sorry," she said.

Sandy slammed the blade of the hatchet into Jeff's neck. Andrew screamed in horror and ran towards the duo.

The blade sliced deep into Jeff's neck severing his windpipe and cutting into his carotid artery. Blood gushed from the wound, spilling into his open throat. His instinct was to clutch at it, but his hands were bound. The blood gushed down his throat and he began to cough.

Liquid began to fill his lungs and he slumped over to allow the gushing to fall onto the pale marble.

Sandy grabbed the ax near his leg and stood up. Andrew rushed Sandy and dove at her like he was tackling a football player. He hit her in the mid-section just as she was bringing down the ax. It swung, nearly missing him, and the impact of the blow caused her to drop it on the floor.

Sandy crashed to the hard marble with Andrew landing on top of her. She struggled to get him off of her, but his hand found her neck and gripped it tightly. She screamed out and began wilding throwing her fists in the air.

Andrew gripped her neck with his good

hand as his other arm flailed around trying to avoid Sandy's blows. She landed one on the side of his face, but it wasn't hard enough to disorient him.

Sandy grabbed Andrew's injured shoulder and twisted it. Andrew screamed in pain and released Sandy's neck.

She kneed him in the groin and Andrew fell off, clutching his shoulder in pain. His head hit the frozen white marble and pain shot throughout his body.

Sandy jumped off of him and ran for the ax. She jumped over Jeff's legs and grabbed it by the handle. Jeff laid on the floor, still bleeding. The choking seemed to have stopped. Sandy wondered if he was still breathing as she stepped back over him towards Andrew.

Andrew rolled over on his back to find Sandy standing over him with the ax.

"You should have just stayed home, Andrew," she said to him.

Andrew put his arm in front of his face to shield him from the blow. He cringed and held his breath waiting for it.

Sandy raised the ax high above her head and prepared to bring it down. She focused on Andrew's arm and aimed for the center of his head. Just as she was about bring it down when a sharp pain hit her in the leg, knocking her center of balance off. As she fell, she looked down and saw Jeff's boot. He wasn't dead at all, he had just kicked her and saved Andrew's life.

She hit the floor with a thud, slamming her shoulder into the marble. She let out a yelp and immediately jumped back up. Before Andrew even had a chance to react, Sandy grabbed the ax and ran back down the marble hallway.

Andrew watched as Sandy retreated down the hallway towards the office. He crawled over to Jeff. His head was still spinning from the fall and it would not allow him to stand yet.

"Jeff," Andrew whispered, grabbing his hand.

Jeff used the little strength he had left to turn to Andrew. Blood was still gushing from the wound in his neck. It had started to dry on his shirt and form a perfectly shiny red round pool on the marble floor.

"I'm sorry," Jeff whispered to Andrew.

"It's not your fault Jeff. None of us could have known about this."

"I let you all down," Jeff responded.

Andrew began to tear up.

"There's an exit behind the cedar plank wall," Jeff said.

"Don't try to talk," Andrew said, realizing that it was futile anyway. "Save your strength."

Jeff looked him in the eye. It was a cliché, but thoughts and memories throughout his life came flooding back to him. He thought of drinking beers in college with Eddie. He thought of building his dream home with no one to share it with. He thought of this dying business. He thought of Sandy. He had let her down most of all.

But, in the final moments of Jeff's life, none of this mattered. He had accepted it all and allowed the cold chill from the marble embrace his body and send him off into death.

31

Andrew walked with the hatchet firmly gripped in his hand. He was going to make it to the exit and he wasn't going to let Sandy surprise him. He didn't notice where she ran off after killing Jeff, but he realized she couldn't have gone far. He assumed she was hiding in the office.

He approached the office door with caution. He stood outside of it listening for any sign of life inside.

Through the doorway he could see the

demolished bathroom door and Amanda's body pinned next to it.

Andrew took another step and he was only a few inches away from the door. He leaned slightly and looked inside. He could see the demolished cedar plank wall, but there were no signs of Sandy.

He braced the hatchet in front of himself and stepped into the office.

It was empty.

Sandy was nowhere to be found. He quickly hurried over to the cedar plank wall and dropped to his knees. He climbed through the hole that Jeff and Amanda had made and stood in the darkness behind the wall.

Andrew allowed his eyes a moment to adjust to the darkness behind the wall. He began to see outlines and shapes before he remembered that he still had Jeff's cell phone in his pocket. He pulled it out and found the settings menu. He changed the screen saver setting to "never" and placed the phone on the ground below him.

The phone gave off and eerie blue glow. He started on the left side of the room and scanned towards the right. He was having difficulty making anything out. He continued sweeping his eyes to the right and finally found the door that Jeff warned him about.

Andrew breathed a sigh of relief. He wasn't out yet, but at least he had found the exit.

He was determined, even if he had to chop the door down with the hatchet, to get out of the mausoleum for good.

He noticed something else beside the door. It was shiny and silver. The glow from the cell phone reflected it back at Andrew. He squinted to try to get a better look at it. He leaned forward, trying to figure out what it was.

The shadow began to change, and the glare hit the object at a different angle. Only as it was flying towards his head did Andrew realize that it was the blade of the ax.

He ducked just in time and fell to the floor. Andrew heard the ax hit the wall and he scrambled to get away from it before Sandy had another chance to strike.

Sandy grunted and screamed out, "you're not going to make it out of here alive."

She had just missed Andrew's head by an inch and the force at which she had swung the ax drove it deep into the wall. She pulled at the handle but it wouldn't budge.

Andrew bumped into something and quickly realized it was Sandy's leg. He crawled back slightly and pushed forward again quickly, this time hitting Sandy's leg with some force.

The hit knocked Sandy off balance and sent her falling backward directly into the wall of razor wire that she had set up.

Pain shot throughout her body as the sharp bladed edges pierced her skin from the base of her neck down to her legs. She screamed out and Andrew only then realized that the razor wire was there.

Sandy attempted to regain her balance, but she was placing too much weight on the wire. Without something to grab onto, she was quickly sliding down the wire, each blade slicing into her skin like a knife through a marshmallow.

Knowing she had to do something to stop her slow agonizing descent, Sandy grabbed onto one of the rows of wire.

One of the razors sliced into her hand as she attempted to leverage her weight and regain her balance. She pulled herself up with the razor slicing deeper and deeper into her hand.

She screamed out in pain as the razor sliced into the ligaments in her hand. But, it was worth the pain, she stopped herself from sliding down the wire wall and regain her balance. She brought herself to her feet and quickly searched around for Andrew. She found him crawling back under the cedar plank wall, trying to get back out into the office.

Sandy reached down and grabbed him by the leg. Andrew let out a yelp and started to squirm. He was more than halfway out into the office before he felt Sandy grab his ankle.

He immediately let go of the hatchet and began flailing his good arm, looking for something to grab onto.

Sandy pulled hard on his ankle and began yanking him back into the room.

Andrew's hand found one of the boards that Jeff and Amanda had pulled off of the cedar wall. He gripped on to it and hoped it would allow him to pull himself out into the safety of the office. But, the board began to move. It wasn't attached to anything. But, it did have a few nails protruding from the end of it.

Andrew drug the board as it was pulled back behind the cedar wall with him.

Before he knew it, he was back behind the cedar wall in the darkness illuminated only by the pale blue glow of Jeff's cell phone. His arm was still in the office, firmly gripped on the board, out of Sandy's sight.

Sandy reached down and grabbed Andrew by the hips, flipping him over. She gave him a quick kick in the groin and Andrew groaned in pain. She was ruthless. She needed to buy herself a few seconds to get the ax out of the wall.

She stepped over and gripped it by the handle. Andrew watched through a haze of pain, unable to move, or even breathe.

Sandy grabbed the ax by the handle and yanked with all of her might. The ax came free, bringing a cloud of dust and debris with it.

Andrew saw all of the cuts that the razor wire left on Sandy. She was bleeding from several spots on her neck, her arms, and the backs of her legs. He couldn't tell what injuries she suffered on her back, but her hand still pumping a continuous stream of blood. She wasn't closing it all the way, so Andrew figured she must have hurt it pretty badly.

She was years away from the Sandy he knew.

"Please," he once again begged. "I didn't have anything to do with this."

She contemplated this for a minute. "But you know about it, that's all that matters."

"Sandy, I'm sorry about what happened to Eddie." Sandy cringed just hearing his name. "But, none of this is going to bring him back."

"Shut up," Sandy instructed, twisting her hand around the handle of the ax.

"He's gone now, you have to pick up the pieces and move on.

"This is my final step in moving on," Sandy said, raising the ax above her head.

"Sandy," Andrew screamed.

She breathed in and looked Andrew in the eye. Andrew knew it was his last chance. He pulled the board into the office and swung it at Sandy's midsection. She didn't even have time to respond. Andrew caught her off guard and she nearly dropped the ax.

The air was taken out of her lungs and Sandy tried to suck it back in. She looked down to find the board stuck in her rib cage. The nails in the end of it stuck firmly between her ribs, puncturing her right lung. Sandy again tried to breath in, but only seemed to suck in pain.

She let out a yelp and dropped the ax behind her head. It fell against the razor wire and bounced to the ground. She grabbed for the board. As her hands found it and she attempted to grab it, the nails in her side drove further into her lung. Sandy made a feeble attempt to pull it out, but the small movement scraped the nail against her rib bone and she froze.

Andrew saw this as his chance. He lifted his legs and pulled them back to his chest. He thrust them forward with all of his strength and hit directly on the board in Sandy's chest.

This drove the nails even deeper into Sandy's lung and the pain shot throughout her body causing her to lose her balance. This time, instead of falling on the razor wire, Sandy fell through it.

The force at which Andrew kicked her, threw her back, pulling the razor wire out of its resting place, entangling her in it on her way down to the floor.

Sandy yelped again in agony as Andrew saw a cleared path to the exit door. He jumped to his feet as the room began to spin. He stood up too fast, but didn't allow this to stop him.

He rushed past Sandy towards the door, carefully avoiding the dangling razor wire all around him. He misjudged his step and once again hit the board protruding from Sandy's side. This time, the force with which he hit it, pulled it quickly from Sandy's side.

Andrew could hear the horrible scraping sound of metal on bone as the nails withdrew from Sandy's ribcage. He looked down to see a horrible crimson wound in Sandy's side as she reached to clutch it.

He heard a gurgling sound and found Sandy having trouble breathing laying on the ground. Andrew refocused on the exit door and took another step. This time, the razor wire was caught on his boot and it began to drag behind him. He shook his leg to get it off, but it was caught on his pants.

Andrew took another step and the razor wire dragged behind it. It was tangled around Sandy's arm and Andrew's step pulled it tight around her wrist and forearm. He took another step and the wire sliced deep into Sandy's flesh and the tendons in her wrist.

Sandy inhaled some air and it felt cool in her chest. The burning sensation she felt earlier was starting to fade.

Andrew tugged his leg again to free himself from the razor wire. The wire dug deeper into Sandy's arm. She screamed in agony, but Andrew felt nothing. At this point, any sympathy he had for her was gone.

It was kill or be killed.

Andrew took a step back to allow some slack in the razor wire. He bent over and tugged at it, freeing it from his pant leg. He carefully lifted his leg out of it and took a free step to the door.

He glanced back down at Sandy. Her arm was still entangled in the razor wire and Andrew could see her lying in what looked like a bed of it. Her lung was bleeding creating a pool of blood that almost looked green in the pale blue light of the cell phone. He saw Sandy's free hand looking around on the ground for the ax. Andrew took a step back towards her, stepped over her injured chest, and kicked the ax away. It slid back under the cedar wall and into the office.

Sandy grasped for Andrew's leg. She found it and attempted to knock him off balance, but it was clear to Andrew she was injured and losing her strength.

Andrew easily shook his leg free and crouched down next to Sandy. He looked over and met her eyes. It was clear that now she was not only in mental agony, but in physical.

He grabbed the razor wire and carefully began to untangle it from her arm. He started at the wrist, carefully removing it from between two tendons. As it pulled it from her skin, blood ran down her arm, pooling on the floor. He moved his way up her arm and pulled it off of her, trying to do the least amount of damage possible.

She looked over and met him in the eye.

"Thank you," she whispered, barely able to speak.

Andrew carefully placed his hands on the wire, between razors, about a foot apart.

"You're welcome," he said softly.

Sandy looked away as Andrew positioned himself behind her and placed one hand on each side of her head, with the razor wire positioned only an inch away from her throat. He took a deep breath and pulled backwards as hard as he could.

The razor wire caught Sandy in the middle of her throat and dug into her flesh. Andrew as unable to pull with much strength with his left arm, so the right side bled faster.

Sandy did not fight him. She let the blood from her wounds fill her throat. Her body urged to cough it out, but Sandy willed it to stop and allow the blood to fill her only working lung.

She was unable to fight the coughing any more and began to violently expel the blood.

Andrew pulled harder.

Her legs flailed and kicked the air.

The oxygen left her body.

Sandy closed her eyes and thought of Eddie. She longed to see him again.

Sandy coughed one final time, sending blood spurting up directly into Andrew's face.

Her body fell still.

Andrew released the razor wire and sat with Sandy's head on his lap.

He took a deep breath and flopped her head off to the side.

Andrew stood up and walked over to the exit. He pushed the emergency bar on the door, and it flew open.

Cold air rushed into the small room. It was dusk outside and the sun peeked over the tree tops, taunting Andrew with its warmth.

The weather report was right. The snow had been falling all day. There was a good three or four inches on the ground.

Andrew stepped out of the confines of the mausoleum and looked up at the falling snow. The opened his mouth and allowed some to wet his tongue. It was cold but felt good on his rough tongue.

A siren could be heard coming down Old Pittsburgh Road. Andrew fell to his knees in the snow and allowed it to wash away the blood on his hands. Help was on the way.

About the Author

William Phillips was born and raised in New Castle, Pennsylvania. He attended the University of Pittsburgh, graduating with a Bachelor's Degree in English. He spent several years traveling before finally moving to London, where he went on to obtain a Master's Degree in screenwriting from the University of London. He currently lives in New York.

Mausoleum

www.ingramcontent.com/pod-product-compliance
Lightning Source LLC
Chambersburg PA
CBHW061608170626
46811CB00001B/357